Panhead

A Journey Home

Also by Bill Schubart

The Lamoille Stories
Fat People

Panhead

A Journey Home

A novel by

Bill Schubart

Panhead *A Journey Home*
Copyright © 2012 Bill Schubart

www.Schubart.com

Author of *The Lamoille Stories* (2008) ISBN 978-1-935052-10-4 and
Fat People (2010) ISBN 978-0-615-39751-1

Published in January 2012 by Magic Hill Press LLC, 144 Magic Hill Road,
Hinesburg, VT 05461
ISBN 978-0-9834852-6-1

Book design by Alex Ching
Cover image by Erin Wiechenthal

Schubart, Bill, 1945-
     Panhead : a novel / Bill Schubart.
     p. cm.
     ISBN-13: 978-0-9834852-6-1
     ISBN-10: 0-9834852-6-7

     1. Men—Fiction. 2. Motorcyclists—Fiction.
     3. Vermont—Fiction. 4. Ohio—Fiction.
     5. Bildungsromans, American. I. Title.

PS3619.C467P36 2012   813'.6
                QBI11-600233

Acknowledgments

Special thanks to Hope Mathiessen, who helped greatly in the making of this work; and to Ruth Sylvester and Jane Milizia, who enhanced and corrected copy. Additional thanks to Alex Ching, who realized the work graphically. Blessings as well on my ever-faithful critical reader and daughter, Anna. Thanks also to Gilbert and Michael Perlman, sage advisers in this time of change in the publishing world. Thanks finally to Page Hudson MD, poet, classicist and emergency room doctor for his literary and medical inputs.

Table of Contents

In his dreams

He has always been able to fly. The air around him seems to have mass like water, and he feels the air's resistance as he pumps his arms to leave the ground. The motion of his flying is the motion of his swimming underwater and slowly he gains altitude of twelve or fifteen feet and moves through the air as if he were exploring the reefs of some atoll. His dream of flight is earthbound like a dream of running—no soaring heights, no gyres or dramatic dives, just steady work to maintain altitude, like swimming to maintain equilibrium deep beneath the ocean's surface. There is never anyone to see him in his dreams, but he can see others below as he swims through the air.

The sensation of flight comes again to him, but he is awake now.

He's roaring north toward home on Route 100 on his '49 panhead chopper. Route 100 meanders along the floodplain of the Whetstone Brook through the Vermont countryside between two mountainous spines. The valley people can't afford the sweeping pastoral views sought after by well-heeled newcomers.

Their ancestors valued the rich river-bottom lands in this valley. They built their farms along the Whetstone's banks and cleared land up the sides of the parallel mountain ranges forming the diurnal horizons on either side of Route 100 and further shortening the waning days of autumn to less than eight hours of daylight.

Earlier in the afternoon, he pulled off the road to share a few Ballantines with two codgers sitting along the road in a dirt pull-off. The 4 x 8 sheet of whitewashed plywood leaning against a birch tree caught his attention far down the road. In front of the large sign is a collapsed lounge chair. Painted on the sign behind it is a bright blue arrow pointing down at the chair with hand-lettering saying, "You, Having a Beer!"

Flanking the chair, two men sit laughing and talking in salvaged armchairs, holding beers by the neck. A bench seat from some bygone pickup truck leans against another birch tree and a blue cooler sits between the empty chair and the older man.

Paul downshifts and brakes to a stop several yards beyond the pull-off, makes a U-turn across both lanes, and idles up to the roadside oasis. The two fellows immediately hail him and point to the throne beneath the blue arrow. One opens the cooler, fishes out a glistening wet, long-necked bottle, pops the top with a can opener tied to the cooler's handle and hands it to Paul as he kills the 74- cubic inch engine.

"Ride like that'll dry a man out. Have a seat and a brew."

"Thanks, I could use a cold one. What do I owe ya?"

"Public service of Leicester Gore ... our welcome wagon for visitors. Have a seat. Where ya from? Where ya headed?"

Paul takes a long swig and drops into the comfort of the collapsed chair, a welcome change from the narrow seat bolted onto the panhead's hardtail frame.

"Driving back home from Ohio, used to live up in Westmore, got another ninety miles to go before it gets too dark. Lights and wiring on this hog's a bit iffy. You guys out here all summer?"

"Weather permitting. The 28 residents of Leicester Gore tolerate us ... call us the Leicester Economic Development Authority. I'm Bub Thompson and this 'ere's Luther Leavitt."

The three chat for about twenty minutes, the older pair asking Paul about his travels, especially his time working construction in the Midwest and his year of college. Passing drivers wave or do a double-take. A rusting Dodge pickup slows and pulls in.

"Someone else's turn for your kindness," says Paul, rising from the chair and remounting his bike. "Sure I can't pay you something?"

"Our social security at work ... pleasure meetin' ya. Drive safe and mind the sheriff in the next town. He's a peckerhead and a teetotaler ... dangerous combination."

Paul kicks the panhead to life on the first try and roars off onto the highway, waving back to his hosts.

He can feel the temperature fluctuate as he moves in and out of the occasional incisions of sun setting above the Winhall Range in the west. The chopper's hard-tail transmits every pothole and cold patch to his spine as he slaloms broadly through the road's own rugged landscape.

When the road and the river wind briefly together he can smell the water and feel the airborne moisture imparted by its cascades. Passing a hayfield with its last cutting waiting in neatly tedded rows for the baler, the smell of new-mown hay inundates him with images of home. He has another two hours to Westmore and he worries about the panhead's ad hoc wiring and the intermittent blinks from the headlight's bulb. He wants to sleep in his own bed.

In the chill shadow of the mountain, he passes through a shambles of a farm. The barn and house are on opposite sides of the road. In the century before, when the farm was new, the dirt track's warp between the house and barn had been a boon, but as the occasional horse and wagon gave way to a continuum of cars and trucks, the weft of family and farm animals across the heavily traveled thoroughfare makes farming here difficult and dangerous.

The roofline of the barn mimics the swayback of the ancient Belgian munch–ing downed apples in a corner of the shaded field. Jersey heifers stare at him dolefully as he roars by. Rusted farm equipment litters the field adjacent to a collapsed lean-to with an iron-wheeled red tractor and rotted out manure spreader still inside waiting to be rescued. The air is redolent with the rich smell of old manure and his mind again races home, and he wonders what he will see there when he gets there.

As he crests a steep rise into the last rays of sunshine, he sees a raccoon waddling across the road, its weight shifting ponderously from side to side. There is no sudden veering on a motorcycle. In the brief second before the narrow front tire at the end of its extended fork hits the raccoon's mass, he notices its monumental size. "Twenty pounds," he thinks.

He is again flying, but there is still light in the sky and he is not moving his arms in a breaststroke motion. He is soaring with his arms at his side. He hits the cold pavement with his shoulder and forehead and hears the bike grinding down the asphalt on its side, the engine still running. He sees the ridgeline of the mountains to the west and the extraordinary contrast of radiant sunlight and black clouds, and then passes out from the pain.

1962

He cannot pronounce the breed of hen he is holding in his small arms. She is content nesting in his lap. She looks away, disturbed only by his sneeze from the dust in the chicken coop's air. It's visible in the shaft of light coming in from the cobwebbed window above. The hen makes contented burbling noises from deep within her feathery breast as if to acknowledge her contentment. He is enchanted with the warm, black bird with fiery streaks of henna in her hackle feathers, and asks his sister Glenda if she will lay an egg in his lap.

Glenda laughs and says, "If you're lucky, she will. Ye might hafta spend the night out 'ere with 'er though."

Paul hears his mother calling them for supper. It's five o'clock. Glenda picks up the heavy bird holding her wings tight to her body and replaces her in her nest box on the small clutch of eggs she is hatching. The cackling of her disturbance is soon replaced by contented burbles as she ruffles herself, as if to shake off the stranger and settles back on her clutch of eggs. The hackle feathers on her neck smooth out and she eyes the two children departing the henhouse with suspicion.

Glenda takes Paul's hand as he descends the steep steps to the henhouse and keeps holding his hand as they walk toward the farmhouse. Paul is four and Glenda is six.

Paul hears a siren and tries to open a blood-filled eye. Two highway crows strutting purposefully on the road's shoulder come into focus. They don't seem to notice him, but appear to be searching for something in the roadside gravel. Behind them, he sees the light-infused horizon as his eye closes. He sees the livid contusion on his left arm where his Levi jacket was torn away by the pavement. The pain overwhelms him and he loses consciousness.

Glenda stands behind Paul and helps him wash his hands by holding his hands in hers, as she sudses them both. The two then join the rest of the family already seated at the oval oak table. Mrs. Lefèvre sets a chipped ironstone bowl with steaming boiled potatoes on the table next to an oval platter heaped with brown shingles of nondescript stew beef. There is a gravy boat with a nickel silver ladle. A deep bowl of soft butter sits between the two. There are no vegetables tonight. A stack of roughly sliced pieces of homemade white bread sits on a renegade dinner plate.

Mr. Lefèvre sits at one end of the table and Mrs. Lefèvre at the other. The two children sit side by side on one side of the table; the other side abuts the kitchen wall. Mr. Lefèvre's shock of wavy black hair droops partially over his prominent forehead, and a furrowing nose and chin form the rest of his plow-like features. He is clean-shaven but a clear outline of the beard he will grow in a few years is always evident at suppertime.

Mr. Lefèvre leads the family in a solemn but peremptory grace, "Bless us, oh Lord, for these thy gifts which we are about to receive from thy bounty, amen," after which hands dart about the table with nickel silver forks spearing potatoes and pieces of meat.

Glenda cuts Paul's meat into bite-size pieces as Paul mashes his potatoes with a forkful of butter and milk poured from his glass onto his plate. The creamy raw milk leaves a translucent film on the side of his glass and on his upper lip when he drinks it. Salt and pepper are shaken over everything and silence settles on the table as people tuck in to dinner.

"You like dat bird o yers?" Paul's father asks.

"I do," answers Paul, "She's a good layer."

"You be gatherin' dem eggs heach day, eh?" continues his father, winking at his mother.

"Yes Père," answers Paul without looking up.

"See's dat you do," he smiles again.

Glenda looks sidewise at Paul who continues to look at his plate.

The two have made a secret pact to leave the four eggs under Paul's hen so they can watch them hatch. The eggs are marked with a penciled "X" Glenda made and, as Paul's hen lays new eggs, they remove only those with no marking.

Paul and Glenda are expected to clear the table and the plates of any remaining food or bones. There is a closed bucket beside the sink for scraps that they will bring to the chickens in the morning.

Mrs. Lefèvre stands at the slate sink in her plain cotton dress with its faded flower print. She has two housedresses and the prints are similar, though one is of pale blue moonflowers linked by tendrils and the one she is wearing displays freestanding poppies. Varicose veins now interlace the tendons in her calves and pale curtains of loose flesh are beginning to show beneath her extended arms as she rinses the dishes under the single spigot. The hot water she will use to fill her sink comes from the kettle whistling quietly on the cookstove, not from a spigot.

Her face retains much of her former beauty and her skin, the extraordinary clarity that so attracted Leon as a young man. Her features are soft and harmonize with one another, a sharp contrast to the chiseled features of her new husband in the one sepia photograph of them together emerging from the Barton church after their wedding.

The following morning, Paul and Glenda let the hens out before breakfast. They take turns opening the small door to the henhouse and then stand back together to watch. First, the rooster sticks his large head out the small doorway and jerks it suspiciously side-to-side to ensure it is safe for his hens to follow him down the plank runway. His livid red comb with its freeze-mottled dark blotches flops from side to side as his beady eye scans the barnyard for predators. When satisfied that it's safe for his hens, he struts majestically down the dew-covered plank, followed by his harem of mixed-breed hens picking their way with care. The morning moisture makes the steep incline slippery and the heavier hens often slip forward and cascade into the ones ahead.

After everyone has made it into the yard, the rooster tosses his head back and emits an ear-splitting "cock-a-doodle-doo," after which he joins his brood, now pecking contentedly at bugs and insects. This outburst always delights Paul and Glenda and Glenda notes how close the sound is to the word printed in one of their children's books. Debris and leaves are scratched away to expose the edible delights hiding underneath. The hens gabble contentedly together as they enjoy breakfast.

Once Paul and Glenda have had their breakfast, cleared the table, washed their faces and brushed their teeth, they run back into the yard to watch the hens enjoying their own morning ablutions in the scratched-out cavities at the end of the yard near the barn door.

Each hen settles into one of the dozen dusty kettles that remind Paul and Glenda of the marble pots in the schoolyard where the kids play "aggies" during recess. The dirt baths, though, are bigger, conforming to the hen's feathery bodies.

Once in, the hens flop over on their sides and begin frantically raising a cloud of dust over themselves with their clawed feet, after which they lie there inert on their sides, playing dead. Then suddenly the ruckus begins anew and a new cloud of silt settles on them.

Paul and Glenda's father calls them "the dust bowl refugees," but Paul and Glenda are too young to understand the reference.

Paul hears two men and a woman talking loudly. He cannot open his eyes, nor can he move his limbs. He knows that inside him too much has broken. In a moment of lucidity he hears the three discussing how to "board" him.

"Musn't move him any more than necessary; just need to get the board under him. Mary, can you get the oxygen while we get him strapped in. And bring something to stop the blood flow in his right thigh and left arm. His neck may be broken. Did you radio Barre?"

Paul feels as if a migraine has overtaken his whole body. He is unaware of the analgesic chemistry of shock flooding his central nervous system and attenuating the influx of pain messages to his brain.

He is calm, not afraid, though he worries about his bike. He wonders how badly damaged it is. If it's left by the roadside, it will be stolen and stripped for parts like his last one. He will begin to see parts from it at swap meets around the state. They are moving him now, and the rush of pain elicits a noise that he does not recognize as his own.

1964-1966

Paul is six. He and Glenda are boarding the bus near the mailbox. School buses only go down a road if more than three families live on it. The Lefèvre farm is a third of a mile down at the end of the road in a small bowl on the back of Mount Pisgah. Paul and Glenda enjoy the walk together, except in winter when the road is not yet plowed, which is most of the time.

Westmore has one dump truck. The day after Thanksgiving, Cyrus and Eddie bolt the massive snowplow to the truck's frame and connect up the six hoses to the truck's hydraulics. There are few roads in Westmore, but Cyrus drinks and so must often be roused from the cellar hole he lives in, but it is then too late in the short day to beat the morning school bus.

Paul and Glenda go to school nearby in Orleans. The one-room Westmore Standard School closed four years back when only nine students from town were left and townsfolk were reluctant to pay a teacher for so few kids. Within a month of its final spring, a newly arrived couple snapped up the tiny school and its quarter-acre playground for $1,800, apparently in the belief that the tiny, packed-earth plot would sustain them and offer them independence. They were gone the following spring and the regulation "Vermont Standard School" white paint is now peeling off and litters the former playground.

Like many of the girls, Glenda excels in school. Glenda understands the culture and expectations of the classroom, as do most of her girlfriends. The teachers are women and trained to be fine role models for those in their charge, but the boys in their classes often don't follow women as role models. They choose men from outside the school.

The teachers know from their own experience how girls learn and what motivates them. Some are recent graduates of the teacher's college in Johnson, pursuing one of the two careers available to them—the other being nursing—and some are older women who have taught prior generations, and offer their transient charges an equal measure of authority and empathy. Their experience and pedagogy is often less relevant for the boys, who at this age are anxious to differentiate themselves from the opposite sex.

The school year coincides with the hibernation of farms and the fidgety boys rely on their memories of summer to daydream or nourish other distractions to survive the tedium of a seven-hour school day. They question the value of memorizing historical dates and learning about civics and comportment. Some boys relate practically to the math being taught at this level, but many of the illustrative math problems are expressed in household, sewing and kitchen problem solving.

The boys restore themselves at recess where rugged games like "king of the mountain" in winter or "tag-you're-it" in fall and spring establish hierarchies; or after school on the bus where Spud, the shy bus driver, quails in the driver's seat.

Like many of his friends, Paul finds school difficult. He is earnest, though, and Glenda helps him after supper with his homework, much of which is rote. Glenda and Paul sleep in the same room and, often, after their mother has led them in an *Our Father* and a *Hail Mary* and has kissed them good night, Glenda will review with Paul the new vocabulary words he has been assigned. They do so in a whisper until Paul can give the meaning of all ten words, after which they fall asleep.

In the night, however, the meanings drift away amid the turmoil of his boyish dreams, and he goes to school the next morning in fear of being called on. On occasions when he is sure of an answer, he will raise his hand and wave it back and forth in the hopes of diminishing his chances of being called on later. Paul is like the other boys in this.

Paul's first scholastic derailment occurs with the multiplication tables, which make their first appearance in third grade with Miss Hazeltine. Just before Christmas recess, she hands out a mimeographed sheet with a faded blue grid of numbers in both axes from two to nine. The numbers in the boxes are to be memorized when they return to school on January 3. Glenda, now in fourth grade, learned them in one evening.

She works with Paul through the Christmas holiday with drills from the upper left, 2 x 2 = 4, to the lower right, 9 x 9 = 81. Only Glenda's company keeps Paul on task. It is soon evident to both that no amount of repetition will enable Paul to retain the random numbers.

Vocabulary is easier, as Paul can concoct narrative threads with images linking words to their otherwise elusive meanings. The word "symbol" would evoke an image of a cross on Father Dufault's chasuble at Sunday Mass and he would remember the meaning, though it was often difficult for him to articulate it, whereas the girls in his class routinely fed back the exact definition they had been given on the study sheet.

Paul's best moments in class come in response to the request to, "Tell the class what you did last week," or "Write an essay about what you did last summer." A narrative line helps Paul transpose a remembered event or story into words that impress Miss Hazeltine, though his papers come back to him pockmarked with grammatical corrections—for grammar, like math, is a function of memorized rules and counterintuitive spellings.

Paul sees a dome light occasionally and feels the ambulance hitting potholes and pavement seams. When awake, he is in a Golgotha of pain, but mostly he is in blackness. There is a scramble. His oxygen mask has filled with vomit and the woman is suctioning emesis from Paul's airway, but he is not aware of this.

Before Theron retired and moved into his hunting camp for good, when he still worked for Lyndonville Lumber, he would visit his brother's family on Sundays after they returned from church.

Once, after a subdued Sunday dinner, Theron takes his niece and nephew on an outing to explore one of his favorite places in the surrounding countryside. His sister-in-law still trusts her enigmatic brother-in-law and looks forward to a quiet afternoon in which she can focus on one of her own projects without fear of interruption. After Sunday dinner, Leon takes his weekly nap. His wife, Esther, organizes her afternoon project and Theron, Glenda and Paul pile into the front seat of his rusty Dodge Power Wagon truck and head out. Esther never felt the need to ask where they were going in those days, knowing full well that the promise of a warm supper of leftovers will draw them home before dusk.

Her uncle always makes Glenda sit in the middle between himself and Paul, the larger of the two floor stick shifts rising up between her knees.

"Easier ta shift," he explains. "You got's no ting in da way like me and your li'l brudder."

He then laughs heartily at his own joke while Glenda winks at Paul, who comes late to his uncle's meaning.

"Can we go canoeing?" asks Glenda.

The year before when she was ten, her uncle had taught her the basic canoe strokes on the beaver pond behind his house. After she unlaced her sneakers, removed her socks and rolled up her corduroys, Theron lifted her up and set her backwards on the front seat of his canoe. Wading into the water, he pulled the canoe off the shore, turned it around so she was now in the back facing forward. He then pushed the canoe out into the beaver pond, telling her to practice her "J" strokes, and to keep the canoe moving in a straight line.

At first it was hard for her to determine the degree of paddle rotation after each stroke needed to keep the canoe going straight. Her small arms barely reached over the canoe's gunnels and she had to sit on the far right side of the seat, leaning so far into each paddle that it seemed as if she would tip over. But after several back-and-forths on the small pond, Glenda managed an impressive straight glide back to the shoreline where she was greeted with cheers by the two bystanders.

Paul wanted to try so Theron repeated the procedure. Paul leaned over to begin paddling and on the first effort, the canoe dumped him into the water. Glenda looked at her uncle who waded out into the shallows and dragged his nephew and the canoe back to the shore laughing mightily.

"Who says da wimen's place is in da home, eh?"

Paul and Glenda laughed at the joke they didn't understand. They understood few of their uncle's jokes, but knew well enough to laugh when he did.

"I'll take ya to my secret place on Mount Hor, then we'll go for a swim.

Dere's never anyone dere 'cause 'em Canucks can't drive a car to it like dey can to North Beach—fraids to walk in da woods."

Theron never thinks of himself as Canadian even though he and Leon were born in Drummondville, Quebec. They were raised by their father after their mother died giving birth to Leon. A maiden aunt from nearby Warwick came to live with them in their modest house in Saint-Nicéphore and saw to the boys while their father worked the Jeffrey mine a few miles away in Asbestos.

Unable to make a go of it at miner's wages, their father piled clothes, a few sticks of hand-me-down furniture and appliances into a borrowed farm trailer, hooked it to his unreliable Willys sedan and drove his sons to Glover, Vermont, where he bought a repossessed farm and began to milk and hay for a neighbor until he had saved enough for a down payment on his own small herd.

Leon still likes going to Quebec and visiting the places his father had lived and worked and seeing the few relatives still there. Theron sees no reason ever to cross the border again to his native land.

Theron pulls the truck into a small pull-off by the side of the road and yanks the emergency brake lever up from the floor.

"All out now and follow me. You two can carry da canoe. I brought the old Grumman, dented as hell but light as a feather."

Paul and Glenda each grasp a thwart on the light canoe and follow their uncle down a well-worn path through a stand of large maples until they come to a white sand beach. They set the canoe on the sand and Theron lays the two paddles inside. True to his word, there is not a soul at the beach.

"Now see over dere near the base of Mount Hor, that big rock sticking out. That's where we're going. The path up to it begins right behind it. You two toads ready?"

Paul and Glenda nod as their uncle pushes the canoe into the water. It's not far, but I'll paddle in the back and we'll start with you, Glenda, in the front. No "J" stroke like I taughts you now. We're just paddlin' on opposite sides.

I'll steer. We're gonna go along the shore in case a wind comes up. This boat's like a glider in the wind and I don't go out in the middle with it. Use the wooden trappin' canoe for that."

Glenda clambers up to the front seat. Paul sits down on the floor and Theron pushes off the sand.

Paul looks over the gunwale of the boat down into the water. They are in about ten feet of water and the water is clear enough for Paul to see the freshwater mussels protruding from the sand. As they paddle farther out Paul loses sight of the small objects in the white sand but begins to see massive dark shadows lying still on the bottom.

"What are those dark things on the bottom?" he asks his uncle. "Ol' spruce trees blown down by terrible winds that whip up b'tween dees two mountains; udders jes sank long ago in log runs."

Soon, the sand disappears and there is only black beneath the calm surface of the water.

"Where'd the bottom go?" he asks his uncle.

"Jes passed da drop-off; goes down two hundreds fiddy feets deep, like fallin' off a cliff. No one knows how deep dis lake iss, been sounded to tree hundred fiddy feets b'tween 'em mountains."

Theron and Glenda followed the bouldered shoreline about thirty feet off. Tall, moss-covered evergreens angle out over the boulders, keeping the three *voyageurs* in the shade. Paul continues to peer into the water, but even close to shore, can see no bottom.

"Can dive in anywhere along dis shore head-first and never hits bottom," Theron says, watching Paul, "Won' see nuttin' down dere. Prob'ly sixty feets down right dere."

"Dem cliffs you see on the mountain over dere on Pisgah drops down several hun'erd feet right ta bottom. Hear tell there's man-size eels down dere, but I never see'd one. Caughts me some lakers the size of a small dog, though."

The canoe glides quietly into the broader shadow of Mount Hor. As they paddle quietly, they can hear and then see occasional freshets of water tumbling over moss-covered boulders into the deep water, depositing a small delta of light sand between granite boulders. Paul gives up trying to see into the lake and begins scanning the shoreline, but can never see beyond the tangled overhang of spruce trees that compete for the few hours of midday sun. They are too close to shore for him to see beyond the overgrown talus to the towering rock cliffs above.

As they near the marker-boulder that Theron pointed out from the beach, Theron tells Glenda to withdraw her paddle and set it on the floor of the canoe. He guides the canoe in between a small pile of rock detritus and the marker-boulder that now dwarfs them. A five-foot beach of Cream-of-Wheat-colored sand with sparkling traces of mica deposited over centuries by a small brook gives them a soft landing for the canoe. Glenda hops out with the manila painter, uncoils it and ties it to a spruce trunk as Theron has taught her. Paul climbs out and Theron pulls the canoe the rest of the way up onto the small patch of sand. The forest and boulders above look impenetrable.

"Follow close behine me," orders Theron with unusual seriousness. "Dere's almost no dirt between dese boulders, jess enough for da trees to cling on to by dere roots. If you don' stay on da path, you can fall through and I can't getcha."

He pulls back some spruce branches, exposing the remnants of a narrow, root-webbed path up through the trees growing out of the talus. Given the mountain's steep plunge into the deep lake as seen from afar, Paul and Glenda presume the path they are about to climb will be as close to vertical as a path can be. In places, water has washed away the spare accumulation of soil, leaving only a netting of bare roots as footing. They climb for thirty minutes, stopping every ten minutes to catch their breath. At one point on the path, Theron has to scale a boulder and then reach down and extend a hand to his niece and nephew and pull them up.

As they near the rock face above them, the trees begin to diminish both in stature and branch. Looking farther up to the krummholz far above, they see strange trees deformed by the harsh prevailing winds and rime ice, their frail branches growing only on the lee side of their withered trunks.

The eerie growth and a sudden drop in temperature make Glenda shudder.

"Over dis way," shouts Theron, waving to them. He stands near the front of a shallow, natural cave, somewhat below them and still among the trees. Glenda and Paul approach, still breathing heavily. On the floor of the cave lie the staves and bands of several old casks and remnants of piping, indicating the former existence of a still.

"In twenny-six, dem revenuers bust it all up. My friend Amos brought me up here last year. Only a few of us know about dis place. If it's calm when we down, I show you da coppers in da water."

The barrel staves and the inner cave walls glisten with moisture. An iridescent moss glows here and there in the chill of the cave. A small pool of water fills a natural depression in the rock floor near the back, and flakes of mica twinkle here and there in the shards of sunlight. Paul and Glenda poke among the remains. Paul asks what a "still" is and what it looks like.

Theron's description of a brass boiler, copper kettles and spiral condensation tubing gradually sketch an alchemic image in Paul's imagination, but he will look it up in the Westmore library when he is next in town. Glenda begins to shiver and Theron notices the sky clouding over and a wind picking up below on the lake.

"Times ta go. Doan hurry down. We're gonna take it slow, more dangerous going down den climbin' up. I'll go first in case some falls. Stay close behine me."

The trip down takes as long as the trip up. Glenda falls and scrapes her elbow badly enough for Theron to tie his red handkerchief around it. Nearing the bottom, Paul looks toward the lakeshore and steps wide of the path. His right foot falls through the web of roots and he falls sideways as his leg slips into the gap between boulders in the talus. Theron pulls him back up by his armpits and steadies him again on the path.

When they reach the shore, Theron climbs out on the large boulder and pulls Glenda and then Paul up next to him. The three lie there staring down into the water. A passing cloud darkens the water for a minute and then again reveals the sun. Theron shouts, "Dere, look over dere, you see 'er in the water?"

"I see it!" shouts Glenda.

A few seconds later, Paul adds, "Me too. It's smaller than I thought."

In the sunlight, lying in fifteen feet of water, they can make out part of a large copper cylinder, reflecting the late afternoon sun among the shadowy boulders.

"Can I swim down and look at it?" Paul asks his uncle.

"Anudder time. We got's to head out, it's darkening and I feel winds risin' up. Dis ain' da canoe for fightin' wid dem winds. Let's go."

Theron takes the rear seat and assigns Glenda the front while Paul again sits in the middle on the floor.

Theron tells Glenda to simply paddle straight and hard and that he will do the same, keeping the canoe next to the shoreline. The wind stiffens.

It is increasingly hard for Theron to keep the buoyant craft from going straight into the rising headwind. Theron neither owns nor thinks much about life jackets, though he sees them occasionally on the lake, especially in the increasing number of down-country pleasure boats. Glenda tries to stabilize the front of the boat, but the lightweight canoe, displacing less than a few inches of water, begins to behave more like an errant balloon on the choppy water.

Theron tries to steer the boat closer to the shore, but the wind is as strong there as it is out in the middle of the lake. Mount Pisgah and Mount Hor are often said to act as a wind funnel. Ten thousand years ago, the receding glacier left a steep channel only a few thousand feet wide that amplifies even casual winds into lethal storms.

"Lie down on the bottom," Theron shouts to Glenda and Paul over the wind.

Theron leans forward off his seat and kneels on the bottom of the boat. He no longer paddles, but uses his paddle as a rudder to keep the canoe's bow following the wind. This is not the first time he has had this experience on the lake.

Theron is not a powerful swimmer and the temperature of the lake, even at the height of summer, induces hypothermia after only a short time in the water. In big blow-ups, he has seen four-foot waves between the mountains, but Theron is not the type of man to panic. His niece and nephew lying flat on the bottom of the boat keep him focused on getting safely to shore. Their weight on the bottom, along with his kneeling, adds stability to the lightweight canoe.

The wind continues steadily, propelling the canoe along the shoreline away from the beach. Theron steadies the canoe with his paddle and keeps it near and more or less parallel to the shoreline. If the wind holds steady, the canoe will be driven ashore on Crescent Beach in the heart of the upscale camps where the shoreline curves abruptly to the north.

"Are we going to be OK?" asks Glenda, looking up from the floor of the canoe at the darkening sky.

"You can count on dat," answers Theron, raising his voice above the wind and the noisy lapping of water against the aluminum. The wind increases steadily, though, and the canoe is buffeted more by the wind. Theron has to work harder to keep the canoe aligned with the fleeting shoreline.

"Take us about half hours to get to the beach at dis rates of speed. The winds be doin' all da paddlin's for us. I jes steer dis ship wid my paddle. You keep the weight low like yer doin'."

Fear drains the usual bravado from their uncle's words.

The wind steadily increases and occasionally catches the canoe sideways. Theron has to pull hard with the paddle to realign the canoe with the shore. He hears Paul let out a soft "geeze" once as he grips the gunwales from below.

After about twenty minutes, Theron shouts, "We're almost at da beach. Look up now. When I tell ya, hop over and walk inta the beach. It's gettin' shallow."

"Git."

Glenda rises up, grabs the gunnels and hops over the side of the canoe into waist-deep water. Paul follows her, but the water comes up over his chest. The two dive forward and swim through the white-capped waves toward shore. Theron guides the canoe in a bit farther, then hops overboard, draws the canoe up onto the sand, and tips it on its side.

Glenda's trembling, her purple lips quivering. Paul sits in the lee of the canoe to get out of the wind. The three look back at the white-capped channel between the mountains and feel the cold spume of wind-borne water dripping down their faces.

"I'll have ta call yer pa ta come git us. Ain't lookin' forward ta hearin' from yer ma. She ain' gonna like dis tale, even though we'se in no danger."

"Hardly any locals on dis side o' da lake. Be a bit a'fore I come back. Goin' down to see if Bev Johnson's at camp. She's from Hardwick and she's got a four-party phone. Some still ain' got no phones here."

Theron strides off down the beach toward the cluster of summer camps.

"I'm freezing," says Glenda. "Let's get out of the wind," answers Paul. "There's a summer shed back in the cedars where they keep the beach stuff in the winter. It's never locked."

The two cross the beach into a thicket of white cedars. Paul finds the small cabin lined with mossy cedar shiplap, and the two take refuge inside out of the wind.

"That was really fun," says Paul. "I really want to go back and dive down and see that still close up."

"I thought the cave was creepy," Glenda manages between chattering teeth, "especially that weird glowing moss and the funny shaped trees. Kind of like something out of those scary stories we hear on dad's Zenith. I'm not rushing back there, though the still was interesting. Did Uncle Theron say they made whiskey in it?"

20

"Yeah," Paul answers, "It was illegal. Kids at school talk about people like Uncle Max who made it in his woods or Ronnie's grandfather who smuggled it down from Canada. Ernie in sixth grade told about the Revenue men tryin' to track 'em and arrest 'em."

The two continue to talk in whispers as if they might be overheard.

After half an hour, they hear their uncle calling from the beach. They run out and onto the beach, where their uncle is holding open a striped Johnson Woolen Mills blanket that he wraps around them as they run to him.

"Bev lent me dis blanket to warm you two up," Theron laughs.

"We've been in the beach cabin," explains Paul.

"Good tinkins," laughs Theron.

"Your fadder's comin' wid his truck to fetch us. He'll 'ave to drop me at my truck at t'other end of the Lake where we left 'er. Then he'll get you two 'ome. Yer mudder's hoppin' mad at me, so I may jess go on home and skip dis supper."

Paul is aware of activity around him. A tinny radio speaker barks a constant stream of orders to someone as shadows move around him. The hurricane of pain has subsided into an arcadian euphoria of morphine and treescapes. He is lying on a forest floor looking up through trees at a clear blue sky. He thinks he hears woodwinds.

1968

Paul and Glenda's paternal grandfather has been a widower for several years and when arthritis overwhelmed his ability to maintain his own farm, he sold his herd of 24 cows, his 28-acre farm and moved in with the second generation of neighbors whose own parents had first given him a job when he moved to Glover from Quebec with his wife, Thérèse. The neighbors offered him bed and board in exchange for some modest help on their own farm next door in Glover, especially during haying season. As arthritis tightened its grip on him and his mobility decreased, the chores became tokens that upheld his dignity and standing as a "hired man" rather than a charity case.

Armand's son, Leon, and daughter-in-law, Esther, come down several times a year from their own farm high above Lake Willoughby to visit and take him to the Glover Diner for a Sunday dinner of meatloaf and french fries with gravy, his favorite. Farming small talk and weather news are shared over the meal and Pepère Armand asks questions of his earnest grandchildren. They answer enthusiastically and farther nourish with elaborate stories.

When the "room-tism" confines Armand largely to his room and the grandchildren are older, Leon and Esther come alone to tend to him in his decline. There is no question of his moving in with them, as there's no room and the couple where Armand lives have come to see him as part of their own family as well. Armand often remarks to his son and daughter-in-law, "I'm a lucky man what wid two famblies carin' on me."

In the late summer of '68, word comes from the family caring for Pepère Armand that he has died in his sleep. Leon solicits the help of his brother, Theron, who has shown scarce interest in the care and maintenance of their father in his declining years. Theron agrees to come and stay with Paul and Glenda while his brother and sister–in–law go to Glover to prepare Armand for burial and to arrange a funeral at the Catholic church in nearby Barton.

Theron seems grateful to have a task that precludes his having to help manage the details of his father's funeral. Leon and Esther will be gone for two days and will call back to let Theron know the time of the funeral in Barton. Theron will drive Paul and Glenda down to Barton in his truck, "dressed appropriately for a church service," adds Esther. She nods firmly at her husband as she says this, as it has never been Theron's way to attend church.

Theron relishes his parental role, as he never had children, and, other than an infamous "lost weekend" in Quebec City from which his brother had to rescue him and make profuse apologies to the authorities, Theron has evinced little or no interest in women or their ability to deliver him progeny. Esther believes that Theron finds infants too daunting, as he paid no attention to his niece and nephew until they could respond enthusiastically to his stories and planned activities, like fishing, canoeing, exploring, and, later, hunting and logging.

Perhaps by design, Theron arrives too late to commiserate with his brother and sister-in-law and to get directions from his sister-in-law for taking care of the house and kids.

It's mid-afternoon when he arrives and there is little to do other than heat up one of the two main meals Esther has left in the icebox. Theron looks them both over and, to the amusement of his niece and nephew, sniffs raccoon-like at the two dishes as they sit in the icebox. One was Esther's signature meatloaf and the other, a slab of pre-cooked pork shoulder ready to heat up, slice and eat.

Paul and Glenda try to hide their amusement as their domestically inept uncle finds his way around the kitchen and finally says in mock seriousness, "You two toads set the table for dinner while I heat diss 'ere meat up in th'oven."

The two oblige and then sit down, waiting for their uncle to bring the dishes to the table. After several, loud sacrilegious oaths cached in *québécois*, Theron deposits a burning-hot dish on the oilcloth-covered table. The smell of burning oilcloth mingles with the delicious smell of roast pork and Theron hacks the roast into chunks and deposits them on the children's plates. Neither Paula nor Glenda choose to question the lack of vegetables or potatoes or the amount of salt their uncle empties onto the pork on his plate.

Unbidden, Glenda gets up and goes to the icebox and brings butter and milk to the table and then fetches a half-loaf of homemade bread, a breadknife and three jelly jar glasses to the table.

"Good idée," mutters Theron, his open mouth a snaggle-tooth proscenium for the battle he is waging against a mouthful of pork cartilage. "I'll have some dat milk, too." Theron takes the glass bottle and guzzles a quarter of the contents, dribbling some down his stubbly chin, which he wipes with his shirt sleeve. "Meat and milk, cant's beat dat, eh?"

Paul and Glenda struggle to stifle their laughter and can only imagine the horror with which their mother would have greeted such behavior at her table. Theron then pulls a piece of bread off the previously neat loaf, slathers it with a hard slice of butter, farther mutilating it, and stuffs half in his mouth.

"You mama made dis bread, eh? Das good bread, better'n' a store-bought I gets, eh? Tastin' like cottonballs dat bread do. Eat up, now, so you can grow ups like me."

Theron smiles broadly, showing his warrior teeth and the remnants of the defeated pork sinew, all of which diminishes the formality Paul and Glenda usually feel at the dinner table. They smile as well, still struggling to stifle their laughter at the circus their normally staid table has become. Theron pushes the platter of meat toward his niece and nephew and says, "Have more, put some meat on dem bones, grow up strong like yer Uncle Theron eh?" The movement of the platter toward them exposes a large oval burn-ring in the tablecloth.

"Uh-oh, your memère gonna know who done dat, eh? Finish up and we go see to dem cows and I'll do some milkin's while you two trow down some hay."

Theron is done. Half the roast is gone and Paul and Glenda are still making their way through the hardy chunks their uncle deposited on their plates.

To their stunned surprise, their uncle emits a raucous and lengthy fart, a stellar exemplar of the throttled airstream theory of sound generation in the form of a raucous and lengthy fart. Theron doesn't appear to notice, but his niece and nephew both explode in uncontrollable laughter.

"What's dat's so funny? You never heard *des ratons aboyants* before dis?"

After the two finally manage to get their laughter under control, Paul asks, "What's that?"

"*Des ratons aboyants*.... How you call in H'inglish? Barkin' rats, I tink."

"Barking rats?" asks Glenda, still smiling, but now perplexed.

"Das what you heard a minute ago, a barkin' rat. I teach you how to do it, but don' be makin' dat sound when your memère's 'round, 'specially at da table, she be blamin' me for you makin' dat noise. H'if it happen, you doan h'admits you done it and blamin' it on barkin' rats, you see, and you don' gets blamin' for dat noise and sometin' smellin' bad."

Paul and Glenda, trying to subdue their giggles, finish their meat, sliced bread and milk. They ask their uncle if they may be excused.

"S'cusin' you for what? You din't fart. I did. No s'cusin's bein' necessary. Whyn'chu two toads do up dem dishes and I'll start da milkin's"

Paul and Glenda clear and begin washing the dinner dishes. Just as their uncle is about to leave, Paul farts loudly and Glenda stares at him, appalled.

"Das good, I'ss very good. Dere's barkin' rats all over dis 'ere house. Glenda, see if you can finds one."

Theron's in the barn. His niece and nephew, still amazed and giggling, discuss their uncle's "barking rats," while they finish cleaning up the kitchen and washing up the greasy supper dishes.

"What're we gonna tell mom about the tablecloth?" Paul asks Glenda.

"I guess we'll have to tell her the truth ... that Uncle Theron forgot the trivet and burned it."

"She'll be angry with him," Paul notes.

"No more than she is anyway. This'll only give her more reason," Glenda points out.

Over the dishes and sweep-up, their discussion becomes conspiratorial. "Barking rats," I never heard that before, have you?" asks Paul.

"I can't remember ever talking about farts at all with Mom or Dad, can you?"

"No," admits Paul. "I'm not sure either of them do that."

"Enough about farts," Glenda admonishes her younger brother, practicing her maternal role in her mother's absence.

On the way out to the hayloft to fork some evening hay down to the cow stanchions, the two break out laughing again at the memory of their uncle's table manners and the thought of how their parents would have reacted had they been there.

The next day, the phone rings. Glenda answers it. Her mother asks if everything is okay at home and Glenda assures her that it is. It's clear that her mother is not comfortable with the last minute arrangements and not having crossed paths with Theron before they had to leave. Glenda does not mention the burn in her tablecloth.

She is to convey to Theron that the funeral will be the following day at 2 p.m. at the Barton Catholic church. She gives detailed instructions to Glenda as she suspects that, although her brother-in-law has been to Barton, it was not to go to church. She reminds her daughter to wear her usual church dress, and to see to it that Paul wears his white button-down shirt and black cotton trousers that are folded in the dresser in their shared room. She reminds them both to shine their shoes. Glenda listens patiently, as she knows what to wear to church, but understands that her mother is nervous. Glenda is surprised that her mother makes no mention of what Theron might wear to the funeral of his father.

After a help- yourself lunch of leftover pork, sour pickles and apple slices prepared by Glenda, the three pile into the truck with Glenda again in the middle, and leave for Barton. Theron is wearing the clothes he had on when he arrived, now deeply perfumed by his cleaning of the barn's manure gutters that morning. It had not occurred to him to bring church clothes, if indeed he had any.

If Esther or Leon is displeased with the appearance of their children or Theron, no mention is made of it before or during the service. Theron seems oddly distracted during the service, looking around the church at its sparse fixtures, the plaster religious figures in their niches, and the fourteen plaster castings of the Stations of the Cross hanging on the walls between the stained glass windows.

The closed casket sits on two chairs in the front of the church. A clear glass vase of late summer wildflowers sits beside the coffin: Queen Anne's lace, blue chicory flowers, and yellow goldenrod stems.

The priest, next to his lone altar boy, mumbles Latin from *The Common Mass for the Dead*. Of the eighteen people in attendance, Glenda notes that only ten take Communion. Given the propensity for the usual Sunday congregation to assume that those who fail to take Communion are not in *a state of grace*, she suspects the non-communicants, like her uncle, are not regular churchgoers.

Paul waits for the priest to address the faithful and say the ritual *Ite Missa est*, signaling the end of the service, but instead hears *Requiescant in pace* and the lone response of the altar boy, *Amen*, after which people begin to shuffle out of the small church.

Standing around outside after the Mass, Paul notices that his father and uncle have yet to emerge from the church. His mother announces that Glenda will ride with her and her father in their truck and Paul will ride with his uncle to the burial site.

The Catholic cemetery lies on a hillside on the outskirts of town. Paul and Glenda watch as the priest emerges from the church in his black chasuble, followed by their father, the farmer who had cared for their pepère, Theron and another man they don't know, bearing their pepère's coffin. Three of the men wear pressed suits.

The four men load it into the back of a makeshift hearse that had once been a pickup truck, but has since been graced with a shiny black cap over the truck bed with small windows cut out on each side. The priest rides with the funeral director in the makeshift hearse and the cortege of three pickup trucks heads out of Barton toward a hillside overlooking Crystal Lake. Occasional swords of sunlight pierce the overcast sky and Glenda recalls asking her father what they were when she was little. She could not remember the French term he first used, *escalier aux cieux*, but later explained as "stairs to heaven."

The cemetery is dotted with old sugar maples shading weathered and mossy marble slabs dating from the late 18th century. Many lie askew with barely legible engravings. Others are broken and their pieces lie on the ground. More modern gray granite upright monuments with legible engravings bearing recent dates congregate in a different section of the cemetery. The hole for Armand is already dug. The bearers bring the coffin from the hearse to the gravesite and set it down on top of two manila ropes lying next to the hole. As the priest sprinkles holy water onto the coffin and recites the absolution of the corpse, the bearers pick up the four rope ends and lift the coffin up and over the hole. They then slowly lower it into the hole. The priest steps gingerly to the edge of the hole and again blesses the coffin with holy water.

Paul and Glenda's father takes a handful of dirt, throws it onto the coffin and returns to Esther's side. Theron, looking confused, emulates his brother's farewell to their father and the ten people at the gravesite return to their trucks and drive away.

On the way home, Glenda asks her father who will fill in the rest of the dirt and he answers that it is part of the funeral director's job to see that the hole is filled in and smoothed over. Grass seed will be planted. She asks what kind of gravestone there will be and Esther, speaking softly, answers, "We'll see about that later after we've settled with the funeral director. We'll find your pepère something nice, not one of them gray things that's too big for the poor souls buried underneath 'em. I don't want one of them weighing on me when I'm laid to rest."

Fearful of his sister-in-law's judgment, Theron makes a beeline for the farm, drops Paul off, and leaves without getting out of his truck. When the rest of the family returns a half-hour later, Paul has put his clothes away and is in the barn doing evening chores. He doesn't know how to talk to his father about his own father's death, but understands that he can express his love for his father by reducing his other burdens.

Paul dreams that he and Glenda are dog-paddling in Long Pond and Paul suddenly dives deep down in the pond toward the murky bottom, leaving Glenda on the surface. She is used to this and, although she does not like to swim underwater, she knows her brother does, and she continues treading water slowly until he pops up somewhere nearby to surprise her and gulp in air. When he does this, her brother reminds her of the plentiful loons that inhabit Long Pond, diving suddenly underwater only to emerge many yards away after a minute or so.

But Paul is on the bottom now lying in the murk and looking up the through the wavy, filtered sunlight at his sister dog-paddling above him. He has lost his buoyancy and is happy lying there, watching his sister far above him.

1970

Paul looks like his father, but in him, his mother's soft beauty substantially erodes his father's distinctly chiseled features. Paul's dark brown hair and hazel eyes are from his mother. Home haircuts precede holidays and major sacraments so Paul's wavy hair overhangs his ears and forehead most of the year. His dungarees are his mother's only concession to modernity, as Paul no longer wants to be seen in the bib overalls that brand him as a child or an old man.

Paul is subdued at school. He understands that the ease with which his sister and her friends learn and retain their lessons will never be his. He works hard at his studies, but the lessons do not come easily and answers rarely linger in his memory. This is true of many of the boys. Unlike the girls, their native interests lie well beyond the walls and windows of the classroom ... in the woods, the streams, the farm equipment sheds, and garages that make up the countryside. Being inside the confines of the classroom for so much of the day is a hardship for Paul and many of the other his friends.

Over the last few grades, Paul and Tommy Viele have become good friends. Unlike the girls, though, they choose not to sit next to each other in class as the temptation to whisper adventure plans during class would be too great. They know this, so they sit apart and convene only during the morning recess break, during which they plan projects together for after school or the weekends.

Tommy is shorter than Paul and a bit heavier though he is not fat. His face is round and his eyes are set back farther in his face. His skin is perpetually oily and Tommy will be the first in his class to get acne and the last to lose it. His black straight hair is combed in a shock across his forehead that often covers his thick, dark eyebrows. He has a beguiling dimple in his chin, and in his cheeks on those rare occasions when his life induces a smile.

Tommy lives far away on the other side of the lake and one or the other must make the long trip by bike to be with the other.

Tommy is usually very quiet, but comes alive with his friend Paul. He confides in Paul about his troubles at home. Like so many children he believes his friend has the perfect parents and home life. He especially relishes visiting Paul at his farm. He likes Glenda, too, as she seems to enjoy him and often tags along on their adventures. She is not like most other girls Tommy knows who either keep their distance from boys or feel the need to huddle together in a clutch and tease them from a distance. He does not understand that teasing at this age is a covert form of flirting.

It's the Saturday matinee and Paul and Tommy are sitting in the front row of the balcony of the Tegu Theater in Barton. Glenda is not privy to this adventure, as the two boys know she would try to dissuade them. It will come as a surprise to her but they know she will laugh at their escapade when she hears about it. It's not Paul's idea and he is still anxious about it, but he knows that no one will get hurt, only angry.

The Jimmy Stewart western flickering on the screen has lost their interest for the time being. Tommy is trying to pierce a can of Campbell's vegetable soup he snuck into the theater inside his wool jacket. He uses the can opener blade on his pocketknife. The curved point won't pierce the tin. Finally, he braces the can on the floor, holds the knife steady with his hand and stomps on the handle with his shoe. The knife penetrates the can and the surprising smell of vegetable soup rises to his nostrils, overwhelming the smell of buttered popcorn. With the can nestled between his thighs, Tommy levers the knife along the rim, making small jagged rips in the lid. The smell gets stronger, but they are alone in the balcony. Paul looks anxiously at the fire escape door behind them to their left.

"Let me know when the scene comes up," Tommy whispers, "then I'll start making the sound. You get ready. Here's the can." They're watching the screen intently. The massacre of the Indians by the cavalry subsides. A cowgirl rides up to the hero, leans toward him on her horse and busses him on the cheek.

Tommy starts groaning loudly and makes glottal choking sounds deep in his throat, as he turns to Paul and nods vigorously. Paul upends the can over the balcony railing swinging it in a wide arc as planned. The vegetable soup rains down onto the orchestra seats below and the two boys bolt from their seats toward the fire escape door. Paul hits the crash bar first and is surprised that it doesn't budge. Tommy tries it as well. His father is a volunteer fireman in Westmore and Tommy knows that fire escape doors are never locked from the inside. But they are.

The two make a run for the balcony stairs, run down the stairs and jump over the braided felt rope across the stairs at the bottom. The balcony has not been open for many years and is believed to be unsafe. Alberto, the manager of the theater reaches out and grabs the two twelve-year-olds by their coats. Paul and Tommy struggle to get away but can't.

The three are sitting in Alberto's cramped office now with its black painted walls full of glossy movie star prints curling around their single tack. They do not see or hear the angry patrons crowding the candy counter demanding retribution.

Tommy's fleshy face still betrays an uneasy smirk. Paul is trying to look contrite. Soon there are six standing in the tiny office. Officer Leriche, Tommy's mother and Paul's father, who left his tractor in the East Meadow where he had been tedding wet hay. Paul and Tommy are staring at their shoes while the adults discuss appropriate punishments. Officer Leriche suggests that charges of malicious mischief be brought. Albert suggests that they be made to clean the theater, apologize to his customers outside, and be responsible for Sunday afternoon cleanup for the next twelve weeks. Albert's daughter Sylvia is now hammering on the office door. She is unable to cope with the strident complaints at the candy counter.

Later that night, a deal is struck on the telephone. The malefactors will follow Albert's suggestion and clean the theater thoroughly with a mop and bucket, apologize in person to the thirteen affected moviegoers whose names Sylvia has on a list, and then continue to clean the theater every Sunday after church for the next six weeks.

"Worth it just to see Mrs. Otis screaming and covered with vegetables under the marquee," suggests Tommy to Paul the following Monday at school. Paul's not so sure. He hadn't expected his own parents to be so angry about the joke. Glenda's giggles at dinner Saturday evening are quickly stifled by a stern look from both her mother and her father.

Esther places much of the blame for any aberration in Paul's behavior on the influence of her ne'er-do-well brother-in-law. She is riven by her belief that Theron incites bad behavior even though he is also the much-loved brother of her too-easily forgiving husband.

Paul senses frantic motion again. He is no longer on a motorcycle, absorbing the shocks of patchwork roads at high speed. He's in a fast-moving ambulance lying on his back. He feels the road shocks less, but they hurt more.

Suddenly, people are talking loudly again, or maybe he has just regained consciousness. He feels a breeze as the gurney to which he is strapped is rushed down a long, over-lit corridor. The vibrating light with its cold blues and colorblind whites mimics the spectrum of his pain.

Doors fly open. He is more conscious of his pain and opens an eye; the other is swollen shut. Someone is asking him questions loudly, but he doesn't know who is asking or what they are asking him.

1971

The deteriorating machinery that litters the landscape of their farm has always intrigued Paul. The free-standing lean-to between the house and the barn shelters a Massey-Harris MH-20 tractor, a manure spreader and the cranky baler. The side-rake, fork tedder, drag harrow, chisel plow, and sickle-bar mower, are consigned to the outdoor elements. His pepère's Willys sedan, in which he and Glenda pretended to go for drives in the country when they were little, now molders behind the equipment shed, along with a defunct hay loader.

Paul overflows with questions for his father about how things work and what various parts do. He loves poking around in the equipment and tracing the mechanics of the farm equipment. Holding down with his foot the tall brambles and stinging nettles growing around the hay loader, he follows the chain-drive that takes its power from the cast-iron wheels and transfers it through a bevy of gears to the alternating tine racks that gradually rake the hay up and into the leading hay wagon.

One evening before dinner, while his father looks on with a bemused smile, Paul explains breathlessly to his distracted mother and sister how the iron-cleated free wheels of the ride-on sickle-bar mower transfer their rotary power to the back-and-forth action of the cutter-bar.

Finances dictate that only equipment in active use be maintained, and then only when a part's dysfunction disables the whole will the part be repaired or replaced. Paul often suggests repairs to his father, who listens patiently to his son's earnest recommendations, rubbing his protruding chin with mock seriousness. After a joint decision not to replace the rusted-out vertical muffler on the tractor as it contributes nothing to the tractor's utility, Paul suggests they slip a large tomato juice can over the rust holes to reduce the noise. His father endorses the plan and Paul makes the repair himself after borrowing a can opener from his mother.

Once, collecting firewood, Leon hit a hidden tree stump not trimmed to ground level and broke a spindle on the tractor's front axle. The repair required several new parts and a half day's work in the woods by father and son. Glenda and her mother endured Paul's detailed description of the work over dinner.

He is being moved again and lightning strikes of pain shoot through the anesthetic cloud, but he cannot articulate his pain. The moans he hears sound as if they are coming from someone nearby. He tries to open an eye, but is blinded by a light that bleaches everything. Closing his eye only attenuates the blaze of light above. He has lost the comfort of darkness. He still hears voices and frantic activity. Is it his mother telling him to remain conscious? He is confused now and seems to have lost the sequence of his life. It occurs to him that he is dead but then how is it his mother's voice he hears? And besides, he's begun to doubt the afterlife so diligently retailed by his childhood church.

In spite of his mother's concerns, Paul often visits his Uncle Theron's cabin deep in the Worcester Woods alone. His mother does not like him spending time with her increasingly reclusive and strange brother-in-law. She believes he is not "of sound mind" and she says so to her husband whenever Paul goes to visit. To her annoyment, Leon just laughs, saying, "Never was."

Uncle Theron had long since left the company of his few former friends and moved to his hunting cabin. He doesn't own the land on which the wood frame cabin sits. He doesn't know who does. He likes to believe it's on state land and therefore his. No one has ever asked him to leave and no one ever questioned him when he built his deer camp there twenty-seven years earlier.

The cabin is accessible only by an old logging road, now overgrown with maple saplings, hop hornbeam, and whistlewood. His car is in fact an ancient Farmall A tractor with a rain roof fashioned from welded re-rod and a canvas tarp. The road accommodates the small tractor when he makes his monthly trip to town to trade. As a matter of habit, he doesn't visit with anyone in town, saying only enough to transact his purchases.

When he first withdrew to his deer camp, his brother and his family paid him occasional visits, weather permitting, though he no longer reciprocated by joining them for Sunday dinners.. Leon would park at a turn-off where the logging road begins and they'd hike in together. Esther no longer visits, though, and asks the same of Glenda. Paul and his father have snowshoed in several times with extra supplies or to deliver a message. Since Theron does not own the land and his cabin is of no value, he pays no property taxes. Nor does his cabin appear on the geodetic survey maps. He has no mailbox or address to receive mail or to identify his existence in these state-owned woods.

Over his mother's constant objections, Paul is his uncle's most frequent visitor now.

Theron has gotten into the habit of silence and speaks only when spoken to, though sometimes not even then. Paul loves being with his increasingly reclusive and eccentric uncle.

When he moved to the woods for good, Theron started building a sugarhouse to supplement his income. The unfinished building sits a few hundred feet from the house in a cathedral of ancient sugar maples. Unlike the common, double-pitched, arch-ended sugarhouse, Theron's is a single-pitch lean-to with two sides and the rear enclosed. He plans to add a fourth wall along the front with a sliding-track barn door and barn-sash window after installing the firebox, evaporator and arch inside. He will build the final wall only to within two feet of the high end of the slanting roof and well under its overhang to allow smoke and steam to escape.

Theron searched the countryside for a used evaporator, but was unable to find one he could afford. He furtively searched every abandoned sugarhouse he knew or heard of in the county, but could not find one with a theft-worthy evaporator or with any evaporator at all. In an abandoned sugarworks near East Charleston, he found a badly corroded English tin boiling pan well beyond repair, but also discovered an abandoned firebox. The wood-feed door castings broke, though, as he hauled it out of the woods on his stone boat.

Frustrated, he pilfered a massive cast iron cauldron from someone's front yard in Eden Mills, unceremoniously dumping the profusion of white geraniums on the lawn and managing to get the empty cauldron into his truck with his come-along. He escaped unnoticed as the widower inside was deaf. After grinding out the cauldron's pitted interior with a power grinder he borrowed from his friend Max who did body work, Theron rubbed the shiny surface inside with mineral oil, and set the whole over an ash fire, rotating it periodically to season it.

Theron boils sap into syrup using his cauldron and four cords of wood. He has amassed a bevy of tin buckets and taps stolen from maple groves throughout the county. The only other inhabitant of the neglected sugarhouse is a 1938 Harley-Davidson Sport Solo with a seized-up 74-inch flathead V-twin engine. It sits in a corner leaning against the moldering woodpile. There is no chain linking the transmission and the rear wheel, and the spring-loaded brown leather saddle has been eaten away by foraging critters who share the sugarhouse.

"Gonna fix 'er up one day and ride 'er straight to hell," Theron tells Paul and Glenda at a time in their childhood when their vision of hell leaves them with no insight as to why Theron would choose that place as a motorcycle destination.

Paul evinces interest in the old cycle and haunts Theron with questions about its various workings. During these times, Glenda amuses herself imagining how pretty the old cauldron would look out front of Theron's cabin filled with flowers.

But Theron never looked much like his brother Leon. He is shorter by several inches and rangier. His facial features, similarly sharp, have become aquiline with age. He has not cut his hair nor shaved now for several years since moving into the woods and his gray hair touches his shoulders. Neither Theron nor his brother will die bald, as neither shows any sign of hair loss in his late forties.

Paul and Glenda are always amused by the square red lumber pencil nested horizontally in their uncle's long beard, a quirk he has maintained since working at Lyndon Lumber where he was a lumber estimator.

Theron's bib overalls will last him the rest of his life. The occasional chainsaw or battery acid mishap is easily stitched up or patched with a curved meat needle and twine he has stashed in his cabin for when he butchers his fall venison. In winter, Theron wears his red-and-black checked wool shirt over his overalls and thermal long johns. When the weather warms, he wears bib overalls and long johns, which serve as underwear, pajamas and above-the-waist summer wear. A flannel shirt hangs next to the wood stove that he sometimes puts on when the evenings are cooler, but it's missing half of one sleeve.

Theron is more responsive to his nephew than to others. Paul and Theron are alone now and splitting wood for the oncoming winter. Theron is more responsive to his nephew than to others and Paul notices that some of his uncle's chest hairs have grown through his threadbare undershirt. Paul asks him what town they're in.

"Used to be Brownington, but now it's Charleston, I think. Orleans's closer than Barton, though Barton used to be closer. The roads git moved around a lot. Used to take me an hour in summer to get to Barton when it was only fourteen miles from here, but now that it's twenty-two miles, takes longer. I never go above second gear now, too many cars, goin' too fast."

Paul neither follows nor questions his uncle's logic about the changing distances between his cabin and the surrounding towns.

Theron is deliberate about his woodpiles. The lengths must be precise. He periodically inspects the wood Paul is splitting, correcting him if the splits are not "arm-width."

Theron has no heating stove. He heats only with a cookstove. Its small firebox accommodates only small splits or "biscuit wood" as he calls it. A half-cord of wood is stacked inside the cabin, well behind the iron sink and cookstove. The other five cords are stacked on a corduroy of cedar logs next to the cabin under sheets of salvaged roofing tin. When snow begins to fall there's a woodpile twenty feet wide, eight feet deep and four feet high. This assures Theron that he will have enough wood to get through a long winter. He replenishes his pile inside daily from his pile buried under the snow outside. The heat from the cabin drives out any remaining moisture from the wood, he explains to his nephew.

As Paul gets older and spends more time with his uncle, he begins to notice logical anomalies in his uncle's observations. Theron will offer a terse statement on some subject after long moments of quiet during a shared task such as splitting wood, gathering pine bark and cones from the forest floor as tinder to start fires, fishing for browns in the creek, or hauling water from it to replenish the cast-iron cistern above the sink.

One day while opening a path to a newly discovered blackberry patch, Theron announces to his nephew that storage tanks, regardless of their contents, should always be kept full. Paul has seen that his uncle replenishes the water in the 20-gallon cistern above the sink after using only a quart to make coffee. He will refill the one-pint tank on his Pioneer chainsaw after felling and bucking up a single maple. On his uncle's rare trading trips to town, Theron brings a five-gallon can of gasoline and stops his tractor every few miles to top off the tank. At thirteen, Paul notices the difference between how and when his parents manage their supplies, and he asks his uncle, "Why do you keep everything so full-up?"

"Musn't ever run out. Bad planning, bad weather means bad things."

Although the logic of Theron's response eludes him, Paul understands that his uncle's answers are final and that solitude frees him from any burden of explanation.

On one visit when Paul is still thirteen, Theron gives his nephew one of his double-headed axes. This gift is "a sign of mental decline" according to Paul's mother. But to Paul the axe is his most treasured gift and to be sure it is not taken from him, he leaves it at his uncle's cabin for safekeeping. His uncle shows him how to oil it after each use and tells him to leave the oily cloth wrapped around the blade. He shows him how to file the edges differently so that one edge will be less sharp for splitting and groundwork and the other keener for hewing and felling.

Even more than his father, Paul appreciates Theron, if not for the deteriorating logic underlying his myriad fears and lonesome existence, for the imagination and industry that he brings to his hard scrabble survival in the woods. Paul does not measure his uncle by the conventional standards against which rural folk assess their neighbors or tight-knit families assess their kin, and this makes Paul one of the few welcome in his uncle's cabin.

Someone is holding his arm firmly. He can see a nurse homing in on his forearm with a needle connected to a tube. The light above is blinding and he closes his one eye. The needle's prick is obscured by the torrent of pain throughout him. At first, he begins to feel warmer as the opiate anodyne fans out through his circulatory system. The flare of pain subsides, but a phantom, dull pressure persists within him as if the pain is only hiding.

Glenda comes to Paul now in his narcosis but seemingly at different times in her childhood. The black and white image of her as a toddler in droopy diapers pinned at the sides with oversize chrome safety pins. She is wearing no shirt and holding a garden hose that spills water into the rhubarb patch. But this is only photographic memory from his mother's Brownie camera as Paul himself is not yet weaned and at this age has no visual recall at this age. The other images are his own recordings: Glenda at six in her First Communion dress looking like an Easter lily outside the Barton church, Glenda, again shirtless, as a tomboy in her bib overalls her forearms deeply tanned. and her reddish brown hair well below her shoulders. She is standing in their father's meadow pointing at something in the distance. Glenda in her cotton underpants sunning herself on the granite shoreline of Long Pond after swimming with Paul, and finally, Glenda the freshman outside her gray stone dorm at McGill in a dark tartan skirt, pinned at her left hip with a virgin pin and wearing a white cotton, button-front blouse with the two top buttons undone.

In Paul's narcosis the pentad of images present themselves as a chord and he cannot focus on any one. It is only on waking that he can see his sister at these different times in their life together.

1972

Paul and Glenda enjoy swimming more than any of their other pastimes. The fields of the Lefèvre farm lie among several forest ponds, though they only swim in Long Pond, a boggy forest pond with endless marshes and an impenetrable alder thicket at the south end. Negro Pond, quietly renamed after the War, lies deeper in the woods, but is too shallow for swimming. It is also rife with bloodsuckers as it is too shallow to support the bass that feed on them in the depths of Long Pond.

Paul and Glenda are walking through the woods toward Long Pond. The forest floor is carpeted with maidenhair ferns. A barely visible path winds through the ferns down to the one spot along the shore that is suitable for swimming. Here the water is deep enough so their kicking feet don't touch the murky bottom as they paddle around in the cool water.

They are powerful swimmers and their mother doesn't pause when they tell her they are going off for a swim, though she is very strict about her admonition not to swim for one full hour after a meal to avoid cramps. Her abiding fear is of the lake below and between the mountains. The deepest lake in New England, Willoughby is legendary for swallowing swimmers, boaters and fishermen when sudden winds come up between the mountains. From its depth Esther infers that if something should ever happen to her children swimming or canoeing there, their bodies would never be recovered for burial, and she imagines this would be even worse than losing a child.

Paul and Glenda are happiest in the water. They swim side by side out into the middle of the pond. Paul occasionally likes to dive straight down and see if he can touch bottom. The pond is rarely deeper than 20 feet and often he breaks the surface with a handful of muck in his right hand that he holds aloft and yells to Glenda, "I did it. See?" The less Glenda knows about what lies at the bottom of the pond the more enjoyable is her time in it. But she has always encouraged Paul's exploits.

Paul prefers to dive off the end of an exposed ledge sloping gently into the pellucid water. He must get a running start to miss the rock shelf a few feet below the surface. The water looks like tea brewed from the underbrush and leaves that steep in it.

Treading the cool water patiently, Paul watches from afar as Glenda carefully removes her jeans and cotton shirt and lays them out on the sunlit rock so they'll be warm when she emerges. She is now in her cotton underpants and she sits down on the rough granite with its flecks of reindeer moss and lichens and, using her hands, she lifts her fanny off the rock and scuttles slowly down the rock face until her feet are in the water. Paul is aware that his sister is taking on the characteristics of a woman. He notices for the first time as she leans forward on the rock her incipient breasts and the curves emerging from her boyish frame. She takes her time joining Paul who is paddling about and whooping at a heron on the other side of the pond. Finally with a gasp, Glenda slides in and breaststrokes toward Paul.

As she nears him, he looks away from the great blue heron lifting slowly off the pond with its feet folded back toward its tail, and he rotates in the water toward Glenda. He is calmed by the image of her swimming toward him. It is as if he is seeing her for the first time. Her faintly reddish hair lies flat against her forehead and farther down, trails in the wake behind her neck. The few pale freckles on her forehead are made more evident by the brilliant sun. Her blue eyes reflect the water and with each breaststroke her lips open and take in air that she exhales and some pond water that she spurts out between pursed lips. Her strong arms complete their sweep behind her and come together under her and forward for another powerful breast stroke. Then she is at his side. He notices that now he must work harder treading water to stay afloat than she does.

Water beads on her forehead and cheeks and the soft space between her nostrils and upper lip. He notices the clarity of her pale skin. He has never seen her in this light. She knows he is seeing something for the first time and says only, "Go ahead and kiss me. It's all right."

He does so quickly, his hands still treading water. She smiles at Paul's embarrassment.

"You're good," she says, and he asks, "How do you know?"

"I know, she answers and laughs.

Paul splashes water in her face and dives down to the bottom.

When he surfaces, she is still there lightly treading water, her hair fanned out around her neck. Paul looks at her and knows their life together has changed and that it will be different from then on.

She acknowledges his prowess and they swim on until they are in the middle of the pond. Paul lies back and floats on his back and Glenda treads water slowly. She is feeling the cold now. Paul does, too, but it is not in him to say so.

Soon, they are lying on the warm rock. The underpants they wear will soon be dry enough to don their clothes and head home. Glenda is fifteen and modest still at school and at home, but is comfortable lying in the sun with her younger brother.

It's cooler now in the woods and Glenda stops to show Paul the goose bumps on her tanned arms. Her lips are blue as are his own. They emerge into the Southeast corner of the lower field where the angled afternoon sun warms them as they walk across their father's second cutting as it, too, dries.

They stop on the far side to examine a tangle of blackberry bushes that forms part of the windbreak, but it is too early in the season and the fading white blossoms are only now giving way to formations of small, pale green clusters that in another two months will be shiny blackberries, which they will share with a family of black bears living farther up on the back of Mount Pisgah.

Paul and Glenda enter by the kitchen. Their father has repaired the screen door so many times that its warped frame no longer lies flush against the jamb. The screen itself has been patched in several places where the corner of a crate of apples or winter squash has ripped a small hole while being carried in for winter storage. Leo, the cat, has clawed two places near the bottom.

Their mother does not like flies in her kitchen. She darns socks, sews on buttons and otherwise mends her family's clothes, so it falls to her to sew the square patches over rips in the screen. She keeps a small roll of extra screen in the pantry for this purpose. Using her kitchen needle threaded with fine wire, she sews the cut-out patch over the rip in the screen. The door is harder to open now. In an effort to get the frame to lie flush with the jamb, she has tied a knot in the rusting black spring that closes the door, but summer flies still find their way into her kitchen.

The smell of dinner awakes a hunger in both Glenda and Paul. "What's for dinner, Mom?" Paul asks.

"Your favorites, meatloaf and poutine. Papa brought back some cheese curds from Magog yesterday as a surprise and I fried up some potatoes."

The meal is a family favorite.

Glenda sets the table. As his mother bends over to open the oven door, Paul kisses his mother on her forehead and goes to his room for a shirt. Neither he nor his father is allowed at the evening dinner table without a long-sleeved shirt.

As young children, Paul and Glenda would watch their mother, Esther, making her signature meatloaf from eggs, finely chopped beef, onion, carrots, beets and a handful of oatmeal flakes, all peppered and salted liberally. They especially enjoyed watching her scoop up a fistful of the unmixed meatloaf ingredients from her chipped brown mixing bowl and close her fist as the red mash oozed out between her fingers and fell back into the bowl. She would repeat this many times until she was convinced that all of the ingredients were properly blended.

Still using her hands, she would fill her bread pans with the mixture and smooth the top with the tips of her fingers. Knowing her family's fondness for this dish, Esther always made a loaf for supper and another for sandwiches the following week.

When she withdraws the two dishes from the oven, she pours off the grease from the cooked loaves into a hot frying pan into which she sifts flour and adds milky water, salt, and pepper. The hot gravy will be poured sparingly over slices of meatloaf, buttered bread, and, this evening, over the poutine.

Leon had introduced his family to poutine on a trip to Sherbrooke, where he planned to attend a farm auction to bid on a used side rake. At Esther's insistence, the trip turned into a family outing and, on the way home that afternoon, Leon pulled in by a hand-lettered sign, *Casse-croûte 'ti-Jean.*

Leon grew up speaking French, learning English later when his father moved to Glover to buy a farm.

Leon's family sat quietly as he ordered for everyone from the proprietor, Ti-Jean Charlebois. Ti-Jean bustled about his small kitchen behind the counter and soon delivered to the table four glasses of milk, four forks and a large platter containing French fries and white cheese curds smothered with brown gravy.

"What's the white stuff?" asked young Paul.

"Eat what's put before you," reprimanded his mother who had her own questions about the offering.

The family tucked into the poutine and the dish became an instant family favorite. On the way home, Leon extolled to his drowsy family its origin, quoting the popular comedian Oliver Hardy. "...a fine mess," he imitated. But in his residual Québecois accent. This, he explained, was how the diner chef in Drummondville had described the request by a customer to add some curds to his "frites" and smother it all with gravy. "Ça va faire une maudite poutine!"

Paul is in a quiet place now, still and dark. There is no pain. There are no shadows moving around him, no sensual distractions at all. If there is activity, he is unaware of it. He's in the involuntary place of dreams. He is unaware of the five people working on his torn body.

1973

In the spring of Paul's fifteenth year, his friend Tommy Viele rides his bicycle from their farm below Mount Wheeler on the west side of Lake Willoughby all the way around the north end of the lake and up the steep dirt roads to Paul's house, a trip of about four miles by road and less than two as the crow flies. He arrives out of breath and asks Paul's mother, who is in the kitchen pulling strands from fresh-cut rhubarb stems, where Paul is.

Esther is taken aback by Tommy's new crew cut. After she slows Tommy down, gets him to catch his breath and gives him a glass of milk with some cold morning coffee and sugar in it, he runs out the kitchen door to the garden where Paul is tilling old manure into the garden with a potato fork.

"Dad's quittin' farmin'. He's gonna auction the herd," Tommy says breathlessly.

"What's he gonna do?" Paul asks, leaning on the long-handled fork.

"Dunno. Said he might try vegetable farmin' or loggin'. He ain' sure yet, said he was thinkin' on it. Means I ain' goin' to college. Your mom and dad still gonna make you go?"

"They're pretty firm on it. I said I wasn't goin' but my dad just smiles and says, 'We'll see about that when the time comes.'

When's the auction?"

"'Pends on the bank, dad says, they're forcin' it. He's behind on everthin' ... house payment, tractor payment. He don' even git the milk check no more, goes straight to the bank. We ain't had much food 'cep what Mom saved in the root cellar. Dad slaughtered a piglet yesterday we was gonna grow 'til fall so we'd have some meat. Been bad, mom and dad arguin' a lot. Dad's drinkin' again."

"Wanna stay here tonight?" Paul volunteers without asking his mother; he knows that when she hears Tommy's news she'll approve.

"Can I? It's rough at home now. I'd like ta."

"I'll ask mom, but I know she'll be okay with it. I'll have her call your mom then it'll be okay."

"Phone's out. 'Spect dad ain' been able to pay 'em neither. I told mom we was goin' campin' up on Pisgah ridge so she won't be worryin' 'bout my whereabouts."

"Could hike into Negro Pond and see if the perch is biting," suggests Paul. "There's that lean-to up there. We could spend the night, have a fire and cook some fish."

"Let's do it," says Tommy excitedly.

The two decide to ride their bikes up to where the logging road begins, hide them in the woods and hike in the last quarter mile to the pond.

There are no camps or buildings on Negro Pond, nor any roads going in there other than grown-over logging roads. The pond, renamed in the sixties, lies west of Long Pond where the few kids in the area swim. The land around Negro Pond is a swampy marsh, rife with swamp alders, bloodsuckers and water snakes.

Around the southern shore it is not clear where the pond begins and the marsh ends, and the elusive shoreline moves depending on seasonal rainfall. What little firm land there is seems to be floating on an aquifer. The north end of the pond has the most distinct shoreline and is best for fishing, as the water is deepest there and perch congregate in the shade during the daytime, feeding at the shallower end toward dusk.

The boys pack nothing but a bedroll, two fish poles, an eight-inch steel skillet borrowed from Paul's mother and some matches in a small mustard jar. They set off about two in the afternoon with their camp gear tied on the back of Paul's bike, which has a chrome rack over the rear fender.

Recent rains have left the dirt road deeply pitted and not all the puddles have fully evaporated. Pedaling is hard and it takes a good hour to reach the logging road. The boys hide their bikes in a stand of cedar and untie their few necessities from Paul's bike. The hike in is only about twenty minutes.

They arrive mid-afternoon and Tommy immediately begins to dig for earthworms using the skillet as a shovel. After he has found a dozen earthworms under a rotten log, the two bait-up and begin fishing off an uprooted tamarack tree lying out in the water. It lies half in the water with its earthbound root mass sticking up in the air. The half of the tree above the waterline is still growing from its prone position. The boys pick their way through the upward branches until they are far enough out in the water to bait cast into the deep end of the pond.

By late afternoon, Tommy has caught two nine-inch perch and Paul has landed a lunker close to eleven inches. Paul guts and skins the fish and Tommy builds a small fire of dry sticks and silvery hardwood limbs on the forest floor. Tommy rinses the fish and the skillet in the pond and then puts the un-boned perch in the skillet.

"Let's let 'er burn down a bit before we lay that skillet on. Cook better in the coals than in the flames," Paul suggests.

The two watch the campfire in silence. Paul hears a sniffling sound and looks away from the flames long enough to see Tommy's chest heaving with involuntary sobs. Tommy looks away. Paul sees tears on his cheeks and for a moment is embarrassed for his friend. Tommy with his face still turned away from the fire, tries to wipe his tears with the sleeve of his cotton shirt.

Tommy's new crew cut looks strange to Paul as he has grown used to Paul's brushing away the shock of dark hair when he is eager, and letting it fall down over his eyes when he is sad—or afraid, which is more often the case.

Paul waits for him to compose himself and then asks," You worried about the auction?"

"Yeah," Tommy answers, "that and everything else. Seems like our family's comin' apart, Mom and Dad blamin' each other fer everthin', fightin all the times over nothin', silly stuff, like how come there's no salt in the shaker, stuff like 'at."

"Sorry to hear," Paul offers, "Yours is good folks, always been kind to me."

"Ya, but not to each other, least not now. People callin' alla time sayin' to pay up and all. I know Dad feels trapped mos' the time. I'me gonna quit school and see if I can git that cleanin' job down at the creamery."

"You're too young," answers Paul.

"Ya, but eh' don' know that."

"They got ways o' findin' out," offers Paul, looking away from his friend toward the riffling water on the pond's surface.

"If I had any money, I'd give it ta Pa, but Ma says we'se way in the hole to everbody."

Paul pokes the embers around and makes a flat surface for the skillet, which he sets on the edge of the flames. He lays a flat stone over the coals lying under the skillet's handle so it won't get too hot. Soon the translucent flesh of the perch begins to darken to a pale white.

"Be done quick," Paul says, but Tommy seems focused on the peepers making themselves heard around the pond. He hears the occasional galumph of a bullfrog and the intermittent hum of mosquitoes joining them around the fire's heat. Here and there, bats and purple martins circle and dive in the waning light, skimming the surface of the pond and gorging themselves on mosquitoes. By dusk the air is filled with bats and purple martins.

"Never be enough of them bats to eat all these skeeters," notes Tommy, briefly distracted from his woes.

"Say that again," exhales Paul, unrolling his sleeves and tucking his pant cuffs into his socks.

"Never be enough of them bats to eat all these skeeters," repeats Tommy, who enjoys the chance to tease Paul about his habit of saying, "Say that again."

Paul eats the large perch and Tommy, the two smaller ones. Paul fishes some cheddar cheese wrapped in wax paper out of his pocket and the two finish that off as well.

Tommy leans back and digs into his own pocket, producing a crumpled pack of Camels and a bent book of matches.

"Where'd ja get them cigs?" asks Paul.

"Stole 'em from Ma. She'll never miss 'em. She stashes open packs all around the house and even in the barn, but the mice get 'em. Now she puts a few cigs in a jelly jar and hides 'em in the milkin' parlor where dad can' find 'em. S'like a treasure hunt in our house for cigs."

"You smoke regular now?" Paul asks his friend.

"Jes fer fun once in a while. Don' like it all 'at much. Still makes me cough," Tommy says, straightening out two bent but unbroken cigarettes. He lights them both with one match and passes one to Paul who handles it as if he has smoked all his life, though this is only his second cigarette.

Paul and Glenda had shared a cigarette the summer before, one that she brought home from one of her girlfriends. It was fun mimicking the actors and actresses in the movies, holding the cigarettes just so and drawing in the smoke the way they did on screen. The actors, though, never coughed or got smoke in their eyes or sneezed uncontrollably, which always dispersed the smoke rings Paul would try to blow. The two lost interest in smoking after that. But Paul does not want to decline his friend's offering and the two smoke with manly affectation and discomfort in the evening, lit only now by the fire Paul has stoked. The fire's heat and their cigarette smoke keep the mosquitoes and no-see-ums at bay.

The fire now defines the only space between the boys. The wooded shoreline has retreated into darkness.

"Goin' to bed," says Paul, getting up slowly, stiff from sitting cross-legged for several hours. He picks his way through the flickering light to the old lean-to well above the shoreline. He unties the two wraps of baling twine around the bedroll and unrolls it along the back of the shelter where the pitch of the roof makes it impossible to stand up. He shakes out the old woolen army blanket and spreads it out on the pine plank floor. He then shakes out the second blanket and a disused patchwork quilt his mother has given him for his bedroll, laying them down over the blanket. He folds his shirt and pants together into a pillow and gets in under the quilt and top blanket. He is soon joined by Tommy who has begun to shiver and still smells of tobacco. In the pitch dark they can see the jewel-like embers below them. A fingernail moon hangs alone in the western sky.

Paul can hear his friend sniffling. He lays his hand on his friend's shoulder, and Tommy's response is to roll over and face Paul. He puts his hand on Tommy's shoulder. He hiccups from the sob and, giving up any pretense, sobs uncontrollably. Paul gathers Tommy to him, offering his friend the same hug his father had offered Paul when he was eight and his 4-H Guernsey heifer didn't even place at the Barton Fair and Paul had broken down in the middle of the stock ring and begun to cry.

In Paul's arms, Tommy gives vent to all the sadness in him. It's as if Paul is holding Tommy's wracking body together. Paul is embarrassed for his friend and comes to understand the gulf between the bravado Tommy displays to their friends and the terrible fears that have taken up residence within him. Tommy seems more grateful than embarrassed. The two lie quietly together in the dark. Tommy's sobs come at decreasing intervals and he seems grateful just to be held. Paul escapes his own thoughts and feelings and imagines what his friend must be experiencing at home.

Tommy inhales deeply, looks up at his friend who has been looking over his shoulder and to Paul's great surprise kisses Paul on the lips. Both Paul and Tommy are surprised and embarrassed and Tommy rolls over quickly, curls up into a fetal comma and goes to sleep. Paul tries to fathom what has just happened with a mixture of fear and embarrassment.

He knows that girls may kiss one another and often dance together at socials, but that boys rarely express more familiarity than shaking hands with adults or waving to one another from a distance. He is perplexed by Tommy's kiss and wonders whether there is something he doesn't know about how boys relate or that Tommy is different. He suspects the latter and falls asleep wondering if Tommy's perplexing kiss has affected him in any way.

Paul wakes up shortly after sunrise. Tommy is busy rebuilding the fire. In the morning light, Paul notices the long scar along his friend's hairline and asks if it was a bike accident. Tommy answers enigmatically, "No, just Pa when I was little."

There is no mention of the night before and Tommy breaks the uncomfortable morning silence, asking Paul if they should "catch a few to bring home?"

The two fish quietly beneath an overcast sky. The perch are feeding freely and the boys reach their creel limits in less than an hour. They gut ten perch worth keeping, but don't skin them. Tommy uses one of the pieces of bailing twine from the bedroll to tie up the fish in a wrap of fern fronds. Paul reties the bedroll and the two retrace their steps through the woods to their bikes.

The next week an auction notice appears in the Barton Chronicle:

> BY ORDER OF BARTON BANK: VIELE FARM, WESTMORE
> Complete dispersal of real and personal property,
> farm equipment, herd, all goods and chattels,
> no reserves or minimums, 8 AM sharp Saturday,
> May 16. Coffee and doughnuts available, BYO lunch.
> See flyer for complete equipment listings or call
> Beliveau Auction Services in Lyndonville.
> Cash, bank letter, or good check. *All sales final.*

No one at school says anything to Tommy. Projecting their own fears onto Tommy's situation, kids talk quietly among themselves, wondering what the Vieles will do, where they will live, if they'll move. Tommy's eight-year-old brother doesn't come to school and Tommy fails to muster his usual bravado, keeping to himself during the school day. Paul tries several times to engage him, but Tommy doesn't seem to want Paul's company. When Paul approaches him, he turns his face away and shakes his head. Tommy is gone from school before lunch, leaving no word of his departure. His teacher marks him "truant" for the afternoon.

Auction Saturday is a cool, sunny spring day. The auction crew has been at the farm for the two days and the Vieles have already left. No one knows where they've gone. The few ladies who know Norma Viele speculate that she and her children have gone to stay with her sister across the Connecticut River in Lancaster, New Hampshire. No one has seen Phil Viele.

By the time the pickups begin pulling in around 7:30, parking randomly around the farmyard, the Vieles' few personal possessions have been sorted into lots on either side of the front door in hopes of conveying enough value to elicit a bid.

A few aluminum pots, cast iron skillets and kitchen knives, random pieces of china and flatware are laid out on a grain sack and marked "Lot 4." Leftover clothing and bedclothes, marked "Lot six" lie draped over the side of a cardboard box so people can hold up items and check for size, holes, or fabric wear.

A chocolate brown Bakelite Emerson radio with a flamboyant gold-painted dial sits on the lawn with a hand-lettered sign leaning against it that assures a possible bidder, "Works Good." In "Lot 2," a small collection of house tools, a pitted chrome electric flatiron with a frayed black and white cotton cord, a few stuffed toys, a leather bag of marbles, and a rusty toy dump truck are laid out like museum artifacts on another burlap grain sack.

A disarray of furniture sits about the lawn. A rectangular, overstuffed chair sits next to three matching ladder-back dining chairs and two unmatched pressboard-seat chairs. The oval oak dining table looks out of place on the sloping lawn, its grainy surface a constellation of ring-stains of varying diameters. Viewed at once, the paucity of household and personal goods betrays a scraping-by existence.

By the barn, a rusty International B with a belly mower and a newer Ford 8N tractor stand side by side. Behind them a motley collection of farm equipment includes a tedder, side rake, two cutter bars, two wood-frame hay wagons, and a haylift with most of its sheet metal rusted away. A chain-drive manure spreader sits to the left with one of its unmatched tires deflated. A display of well-worn hand tools, an ax, iron pry bar, a come-a-long, and a peavey lean against the side of the manure spreader. A single pile of steel shovelheads, a rake with a half dozen bent tines, and two ax heads lie at the end, what the auctioneer will call a "dollar lot."

The cows remain in their stanchions, perplexed and uncomfortable by the break in their daily routine and from not having been relieved of their milk. The auctioneer has canceled the morning milking to "make the girls' bags look bigger."

The auction begins promptly at eight. The auctioneer's ululations break the quiet of the morning. A solitary black Plymouth sedan is parked by the house with a well-dressed man standing by, observing the proceedings and trying to assess whether enough serious bidders are present for his employer to recover any significant amount of their loan loss.

Paul, hoping to see Tommy, watches from his bike. He left home at seven to make the trip on his bicycle. His father announced the night before at supper that he had no intent of profiting from another man's misfortune and would be mending fence in the lower pasture instead of attending the auction.

Paul doesn't need to search the scant crowd for his friend, as there are fewer than a dozen men with any intent to bid. The rest are the bidders' family members with nothing else to do on a Saturday, or idle curiosity seekers with no resources to spend but with an abiding interest in poking through the domestic viscera of others' lives.

The auctioneer sells off the odd lots in the front of the house for whatever he can get, rarely more than a dollar. Adept at reading buyer interest, the auctioneer leaves the furniture for later and draws the bidders toward the farm equipment.

After a brief summary of the provenance of the Ford 8N tractor, he asks for a starting bid of $300. The bidders stand stone-faced and stare at him.

"$200 ...?"

Still, no movement.

"Well, you cheap sons o'bitches!," laughs the auctioneer. "Mike, gimme a bid of a hunnerd. I know you'se cheap, butcha ain' stupid."

Mike's hand goes up with a smile, pleased by the auctioneer's recognition of his parsimony.

"I got a hunnerd, do I hear $150. She's worth three times 'at! Common boys, don't be dumb. Be cheap, but don't be dumb."

Tentative hands dart up here and there until the auctioneer finally sells the tractor at $450, but only after a pulsing chant urging $500.

By noon the equipment and remaining furniture have been sold off and bidding on the heifers and milkers will begin after lunch. The auction will resume at one sharp.

Paul watches the proceedings sadly, keeping an eye out for Tommy. When the crowd has ambled over to the farm equipment, Paul notices the front tire of Tommy's tank-top Schwinn peeking out from the entrance to the hayloft. He goes inside and looks around but sees no one. He whispers, "Tommy, you here?" but hears nothing except the cooing of pigeons high above in the rafters.

"Tommy, where are you?" he tries again.

"Up here," he hears faintly from high above in the hayloft.

Paul scrambles up the wooden ladder built into the sidewall of the barn and makes his way across the loose hay. He finds Tommy lying in the hay looking out the hayfork window onto the crowd below.

"You okay?" Paul asks his friend. Tommy doesn't answer and Paul can see that he's been crying. He tries for a minute to imagine himself in his friend's position and a similar sadness comes over him. He lies down next to Tommy in the hay and puts his arm over his back. Tommy seems uncomfortable with this intimacy and edges away from his friend.

It is several minutes before Paul can get Tommy to even respond to a question.

"They sold all my things." Tommy says. "They even sold dad's radio. Ain't fair. Not like they got any money for it. If I had the measly two bucks, I'da bought it back for dad. Glad he wan't here. Only reason they din't sell my bike is I kep' it with me."

Paul can think of nothing to say to alleviate his friend's sense of injustice. The two lie there, watching the proceedings below.

By 3:30 the cows are sold and the silage and feed are gone as well, including the hay they're lying in. Last to come on the block is the farm itself.

The auctioneer begins his closing aria, "Now here's whatcha' all been waitin' for ... house, barn and 68 acres of prime hill farm land, 42 in cultivation, small apple orchard in the westerly field, good stand of maples for sugarin' and a nice brook runnin' through most of the northern boundary. Plenty of water for stock, and the spring box up that hill there delivers cool, clean spring water yearround. Do I hear $25,000? Come on, boys, don't let this 'un go. Buy it for yer mother-in-law! Get 'er outta the house."

His attempt at humor draws a few smiles, but the bidders already have farms and no one has the ready cash or credit to buy another. Those left remain only out of curiosity to find out who among them might have the secret wherewithal to buy the place and for how much. It's a means of evaluating one's own farm comparatively.

An older farmer, who has bid on nothing, raises his left hand and shouts, "8,000."

The auctioneer drops his arms to his side, thrusts himself forward and stares at the bidder, finally saying, "Jesus, Jake, I knew you did time for stealin', but I thought you'd finally come to Jesus and gone straight. Stealin's still against the law last time I looked. I can't let you have the property for that price. We both know it's worth four times that."

"8,000," the bidder repeats, "Got any other bids? There's no reserves. You gonna sell it or not?"

"12,000," comes from the man next to the black Plymouth.

"Do I hear any other bids?" asks the auctioneer.

"Sold to Horace Milner of the Barton Bank for 12,000."

People begin milling off to gather up and pay for their winning bids, and within half an hour the farmstead is empty of trucks and people. Those who bought small items, furniture, hand tools and odd lots toted them off, and those who bought animal feed, equipment, or cows are given forty-eight hours to remove them from the property.

Paul and Tommy lie in the hay, watching strangers drive off with the familiar items of Tommy's childhood.

"Where's yer folks?" asks Paul.

"Mom's at Aunt Edna's with Dougie. Don't know where dad went ... maybe to Canada to get drunk."

"What're you gonna do?" asks Paul, still looking out on the empty farmyard.

"Dunno. 'Pends, I guess, on what Ma does. Dad's all broken down and ain't much good now that the farm's gone."

"Could stay with us for a bit. I could ask my folks."

"No," answers Tommy, "Yours is nice folks, but you ain' got no room there and I don' wanna impose. I just gotta figure it out and see if I can find a job somewheres."

Paul tries again to put his arm on Tommy's back, and this time Tommy seems comfortable with his friend's touch.

The two lie in the hayloft until the light begins to fade. Paul says, "At least come an' have some supper, I know my folks'd all be glad to see ya."

Tommy gets up, dusting off the hay chaff and the two climb down the ladder. Tommy and Paul get on their bikes and begin the long ride to Paul's. When they reach the farm, it is seven and dinner is done and the dishes washed and put away. Paul's mother makes the two boys each a plate of leftovers and places two big slices of bread onto each plate, bringing the butter dish from the fridge.

"Musta been a hard day, Tommy," Paul's mother says, looking straight at Tommy.

"It was, Mrs. Lefèvre. It was hard to see everything carried off by strangers like that."

"What're you gonna do?" she continues, "You still got two more years of school."

"Hard to say," he answers evasively. "Gotta see what mom wants when she comes back from Lancaster."

"When'll Norma be back?" Paul's mother continues.

"Dunno yet. Soon, I s'pect," Tommy answers evasively, looking at his friend uncomfortably.

"Well, you're stayin' right here with us. Glenda's gonna stay down here on the daybed. It's all made up. You're stayin' upstairs with Paul for a few days until yer Ma gets back and then we'll see," Mrs. Lefèvre says with authority.

The matter was decided, and had been before Paul and Tommy arrived. Paul had allowed at breakfast that if he saw Tommy, he'd bring him home for supper. Mrs. Lefèvre planned the rest.

"Go help your dad finish up in the barn and then off to bed with ya both," finishes Mrs. Lefèvre. "He could use some help; he spilled a bucket of fence staples and was so mad after he picked 'em all up. He could use a hand. He's just wipin' down the milking parlor for tomorrow. Milk truck comes at nine."

Paul and Tommy go out and help Mr. Lefèvre ready the barn for the next morning's milking. Tommy cleans buckets and Paul hoses out milk cans and stacks them upside down on the pallet shelf. Mr. Lefèvre allows as how he appreciates the help. The three return to the warmly lit farmhouse around 8:30 and go straight off to bed.

Paul and Tommy talk into the night. Somewhere in the discussion, Tommy tiptoes over and slides into Paul's bed without saying anything. He thanks him for being a good friend and again kisses him on the mouth. Paul seems less disturbed by this than before and responds affectionately by putting his arms around Tommy. The two hold each other and soon became uncomfortably aware of the involuntary stimulus of their intimacy. Paul rolls over and tries to feign sleep. When he awakes in the morning, Tommy is in Glenda's bed asleep.

The two speak little during the hearty breakfast of Canadian bacon slabs and buttered and sugared oatmeal, allowing others to sustain the conversation, which ranges widely from the overcast weather to what will need to be done after school.

After the dishes are cleared, Mr. Lefèvre returns to the barn to clean up after morning milking and get ready for the milk truck. Glenda, Paul and Tommy head off down the road to meet the 7:35 school bus.

Paul is in the paradox of discordant dreams, dreams that conflate childhood memories with surreal distortions, the meanings of which elude him. He doesn't try to process them, they are just there.

The people working on him review their efforts, clean up, count surgical instruments and sponges, and discuss post-operative implications. Their efforts in this session have only been to save his life. They cannot repair everything that is broken in Paul in one operation. They will need more tests to assess and treat the extensive damage. They will also need Paul to be conscious and articulate for part of the time and to participate in their work in order to better assess the panoply of injuries he has endured. It's still too soon to tell. The trauma surgeon will make no promises to Paul's parents and sister about his prognosis.

1975

In another aborted discussion about college, Paul has openly defied his father. He is walking on the road away from home. It is winter. At seventeen he has never openly challenged or even questioned his father's judgment. A waxing moon bathes the landscape in an opalescent light. A few dark clouds hover in the sky around the moon and just above the mountainous horizon. There is no wind. The day's earlier snow still drapes the hemlocks, their normally upright branches pulled down by the snow into the snow-drifts at their base. A few of the lowest branches have broken from the weight of the snow.

As if to underscore his defiance Paul leaves the house hurriedly, taking only his Levi barncoat and a wool toque. He knows he can't go very far, even though he heard the snowplow turning around in their yard before supper. Around the table, a simmering argument about college boiled over. He declared his intent to get a job and left the table and the house.

There are no other farms nearby. He has made his statement and will walk as long and as far as he can before he returns home. This is his first overt challenge to his father and he does not want to weaken it by returning home too early. He saw the fear in Glenda's eyes, but missed the twinkle in his father's.

The moon dips behind a cloud and the landscape darkens. He hears the familiar sound of hunting coyotes baying nearby. The movement of their barking indicates that they have a deer on the run. Unlike the more familiar yips that simply announce the presence of a solo male returning from the hunt, these are the sounds of a chase. The deer will have no chance this late in the winter. Malnourished and weary, the yearling doe that bounds frantically into sight from behind a stand of hemlocks in the meadow cannot possibly keep ahead in the two feet of snow. Each narrow cloven hoof penetrates deep into the snowpack, exhausting the animal while the padded paws of the coyotes in close pursuit barely break the surface crust.

The alpha male breaks away from the pack and leaps at the doe's throat. The pack goes silent as the exhausted doe falls in place. Her jerky kicks mimic escape, yet she seems relieved to be down. The alpha male executes a throat kill, cutting off her wind. She is resigned though not yet dead. The other animals have circled her. They have gone silent now, anxious not to transmit to other predators the success of their hunt. Soon enough the others will come to feed on the carcass. The animals begin to open up the doe's pale underbelly and share the kill even as she continues to pant. Her steaming innards spill out into the snow.

Paul has stopped in the road to watch the kill. He is less than half a mile from home and has seen this drama twice before in past winters, once when he and his father were tapping maples in early March. He knows there is no reason to fear any of the animals that live on the backbone of Mount Pisgah. His father has taught him to use common sense and to avoid animals in rut and not to get between a mother and her young. He loves the endless small dramas of living among animals. He looks around to note the location of the kill so he can come back with his binoculars and watch the later feeders, especially the red-tailed hawks.

After another half-hour of walking, he reverses direction somewhat reluctantly. He is cold now and his hands are plunged deep into his pockets. He enters the house quietly and goes straight to his room. Glenda is in bed reading and says nothing until he is in his bed.

The two talk for a while about what happened. Glenda is uncomfortable with Paul's challenge to their father's authority. Glenda is eager to go to college and fears only the loss of that opportunity.

Paul tries again to enlist Glenda's support, explaining that he simply doesn't want to extend his scholastic failures for four more years. There is a long silence and then Paul tells Glenda that he can't get warm. Glenda encourages Paul to slip into her bed, promising to warm him up. He strips back the green woolen army blanket on his metal-frame bed and stands up still trembling.

Their beds have white-painted metal frames like those seen in military hospitals, but don't match, as they were bought at different times after the children moved into beds of their own from the hand-me-down, cherry cradle made by Esther's grandfather. The two beds almost fill the small attic room with its steeply sloped ceiling that follows the roofline. There is a lazy window under the roof's overhang at each end that floods the room with moonlight. Paul pulls the cover back over his bedclothes to conserve what little heat he has left there and slides into Glenda's bed.

Paul is grateful for Glenda's warmth. Glenda cradles Paul in "spooning" fashion; otherwise the two could not fit in the narrow bed. Paul has long since given up the pajamas he associates with childhood. Like most boys his age he sleeps only in his underwear. Glenda sleeps in a calico nightie that extends just below her knees. The two talk into the night.

When Glenda wakes at 6:30, Paul is asleep in his bed and she hears her mother downstairs sliding splits through the round burner hole into the Glenwood cookstove in the kitchen. She does not get out of bed until she feels heat rising from the vent that connects her and Paul's room with the kitchen below.

Paul doesn't know that he has been removed to a recovery room. It is warm and dark in there, lit only by a dim bedside light. He is still in the Lethe of anesthesia. His vivid dreams have subsided, but he is unaware of all this. He has no memory now. His body is consumed with the work of adjusting to the five hours of incisions, transfusions, fracture and lacerated artery repairs. It is hard work and offers no guarantees.

That afternoon, the three step off the school bus and it falls to Glenda to check the single rusty mailbox at the end of their road. She removes the familiar milk check and a letter bearing a Canadian stamp.

"It's McGill," she says solemnly to Paul and Tommy. She slips the milk check envelope in the side pocket of her skirt and just stares at the envelope with the unfamiliar stamp.

"Open it," says Paul.

"I'm afraid to," answers Glenda.

"Come'on. Open it up. I'll betcha got in," continues Paul. "Open it up."

Glenda pries open the poorly sealed flap of the envelope and withdraws a trifold letter. She opens it ceremoniously as if she were about to read a psalm in church, skims the words silently for a few seconds and then looks up smiling at her brother.

"They accepted me." she says, her face wrinkling into a smile.

"They accepted me with a scholarship. I can go." She jumps up and yells down the empty dirt road. "I got in. I'm going to college!"

Paul and Tommy, watching Glenda's burst of excitement, look at each other and smile.

"I'm glad for you, sis," says Paul, giving his sister a hug.

"Me, too, Sis," Tommy jokes. "I'm real happy for you. I ain't goin' ta college, I ain't bright enough, but now at least someone I know who is. I can say, 'Oh my friend, Glenda, she's a college girl.'

The three laugh together as they walk down the road toward home.

Even though it is a year away, the unresolved dispute between father and son over Paul's refusal to continue on to college shadows the otherwise luminous supper atmosphere. The family steers clear of the issue, as no one wants to cast a pall over Glenda's success. Paul has tried earlier to resolve the matter by offering his father a vague promise that he would attend college, but wants to take a year or two off to earn some money toward his tuition, as his grades would never earn the kind of scholarship aid that Glenda's honor roll averages have earned.

His father knows from his "postponement" of the last two years of his own high schooling to help his father just after the Depression that teenagers never look back on earlier decisions, that life moves fast at sixteen and that reconsiderations come too late.

Paul thinks he hears a woman's voice talking softly to him, but he doesn't recognize the voice. At first, it reminds him of the lovely, sad voice of the telephone operator he met at college. The slow, vaguely Midwestern lilt is familiar, but he doesn't recognize the woman speaking. No familiar face emerges from the sound. He listens as she asks him questions and encourages him to open his eyes or move his toes, but he hears only the soft timbre of her voice rather than her requests. It does not occur to him to respond, even if he could.

1976

The 22-hour succession of bus trips seems endless, depositing Paul in a place where he knows no one. He introduces himself to his assigned roommate, Danny, who arrives at Bowling Green in a black GTO convertible towing a Vincent Black Shadow motorcycle on a single-axle trailer. Danny shows no interest in him when he finds out that he has arrived with nothing other than a suitcase full of clothes. Danny has everything, though his only book is a new dictionary inscribed by his mother.

Like Danny, Paul accommodates the acquaintance, but so far has found few reasons to nurture it. Danny is a gangster's son from Chicago.

Other students Paul meets on the pea stone paths to and from advisory meetings and orientations seem for the most part to be earnest Midwestern students with crew cuts and slacks of various colors anxious to make their way in the world and to do so with golf bags and tennis rackets, both of which are alien to Paul.

As roommates, Paul and Danny manage their friendship, though they have little in common beyond a love of motorcycles. Whereas Paul's enthusiasm for them stems from sitting on his uncle's seized-up Harley in the sugarhouse and imagining himself banking sharp turns along route 5A beneath the mountain on which he lives, Danny's comes from a year of riding loudly through the suburbs of Chicago on a machine that most boys can only dream of ever owning.

Once a month, Paul calls across the 900 miles to his home. He must dial for an operator to place a call of such distance and the voice of the woman who answers each time attracts him like a familiar song heard outside a window.

When she asks, "How can I help you?" Paul imagines a young woman with straight auburn hair below her shoulders, wearing a pale green cashmere sweater and a darker green knee-length skirt. Her breasts define her sweater. They are not large, but made evident by the sharply pointed bra then in style. Her features meld into a beautiful, if plain, face that radiates a warm smile. He has never met this woman, but thinks he would like to.

To his surprise, he asks her out before he tells her his parent's number in Vermont. This unexpected interruption in her role as an operator leaves her nonplussed, but she accepts his invitation after a brief silence. She has a car and agrees to meet him at the green in the center of the campus the following Saturday at three.

If Paul's mother answers the call, they have a short talk about his courses and what college life is like. Paul asks the perfunctory questions about home: "How's dad? What do you hear from Glenda? How's the price of milk holding? Anybody hear from Tommy?"

If his father answers, he asks his son only how he is doing, not what. He eschews detail, as he doesn't know what to ask about a college. His father volunteers some local news and says that everything is fine at home and on the farm, and passes him quickly to his mother, who waits nearby to take the heavy black receiver. She knows it falls to her to alleviate the lingering stress between father and son.

Saturday arrives. That afternoon at 2:45 p.m. Paul is leaning against a tree in the green. Shortly after three, a red Sunbeam Alpine with its top down pulls up at the nearest curb and the pony-tailed driver asks, "You Paul?"

"I am," he answers, surprised by the accuracy of how he had imagined her. She is wearing an off-white blouse, however, with a maroon skirt and her dark brown hair is cinched into a ponytail. She smiles in the way he had imagined and he is beguiled.

"Hop in," she says and he does.

The tailpipe is gone on her car and the unmuffled sound of revving and shifting up through four gears precludes any introductory conversation. She looks at the road and he looks at her.

As they leave the town center and residential outskirts, she idles back in high gear. The noise from the muffler abates and she turns to him and asks, "Did you think I wouldn't come?"

"No," he answers. "When you said yes, I believed you, though I didn't understand why you'd accept an invitation from a total stranger."

"I've connected you to your mother before. I would remember Vermont. I don't connect many calls to Vermont. I liked the sound of your voice. You new here?"

"It's my first and last year," he answered, looking to his right at the now rural countryside. "My father insisted I go to college. I have and I'm not coming back. It's not that I don't like it out here. I'm just not cut out for this."

"What do you think you are cut out for?" she asked, looking at him directly for the first time since they left.

"I don't know, but it's not college."

"My name's Cindy. Cynthia's my real name, but no one ever calls me that. You're Paul."

"How did you know? You were listening in, weren't you?"

"You told me your name when you asked me for a date," Cindy answers, smiling. "You get fired if they catch you listening in on calls. Jobs aren't easy to find out here, especially if you haven't been to college."

Paul wonders if her peripheral vision allows her to see him looking at her.

His back lifts off the tufted red leather seatback slightly as she down-shifts and turns off the highway onto a dirt road.

"Where we going?" he asks.

"My favorite spot," she answers. "There's a beautiful view here."

They continue west along the two-track dirt road past a patchwork of farm fields littered with corn stover. After the last farmhouse, the road narrows considerably and enters a grove of birch trees. Paul smells water, but cannot hear it. Cindy downshifts again and the car comes to rest on a gentle, grassy slope leading down to a creek of slow-moving, brackish water.

"Hope you like chicken? I brought some sandwiches." Cindy says, turning around and pulling a small basket out of the niche holding the pleated convertible roof.

"I do," Paul says, surprised at her familiarity with him. He wonders if she has had many dates. He wonders if they are going to have sex. He has not had fully fledged sex yet, only mutually experimental manual and oral sex with a few girls from home. He has yet to take the lead in a consummate seduction. Though his desire to do so has never abated, he is anxious about how.

He watches Cindy walk to a spot near the creek. Like a doe, Cindy readies a place to settle in the tall grass by circling several times before sitting down and pulling her skirt demurely around her legs.

"Sit down," she beckons. Paul does, choosing a spot near, but not too close to her. He doesn't yet know this woman's boundaries, only that women have boundaries, and that he has learned over time to respect them.

Cindy unpacks the basket and tosses Paul a thermos of lemonade. "There's two cups screwed on the lid. Wanna pour us some?" She hands him a sandwich wrapped in wax paper and taped shut with Scotch tape.

"So tell me all about yourself. What do you do in Vermont when it's not snowing?" she says, smiling at him.

"You should have listened in. You'd know," he answers, increasingly at ease.

The mocha-colored water in the nearby creek shows no sign of flowing anywhere nor does it make any sound. Birds trill occasionally in the thicket across the creek and the occasional undulating Doppler effect of a passing honeybee distracts his attention.

In a few succinct phrases, and wholly without artifice, Cindy relates the story of her life in Ohio, which she characterizes as boring, though she doesn't use that word. Rarely does she look at Paul as she uses descriptors that have no secondary meanings. Her job is a "job," offering no interest or opportunity.

The one exception in her life is her car, which she describes as a "blowout" effort to "escape" the drab elements of her existence. She bought it used against the advice of her father who felt she should buy a Rambler sedan because "the parts will be cheaper." She uses the word "nice" a lot to describe her parents, her home, her friends, and their friends. "Nice" is the only deprecatory word she uses to describe her own life.

Cindy leans back on the long grass and asks Paul about his life. He tells Cindy of their farm on the back of Mount Pisgah, the lake far below and of Glenda's successes at school and in college. He doesn't mention his friend Tommy. He talks of farm work and the equipment to do it. Her father is a retail bookkeeper and she allows that she is unfamiliar with the farm equipment that surrounds the small town in which she still lives with her mother and father.

Paul's insouciant tone belies his anxiety about how or whether to aggress sexually. He knows anecdotally that some women want to be seduced and that others don't. He knows also that there is no one right way, and that, like being sensitive to a woman's physical boundaries, it is hard to determine the right pace and tenor of a seduction. He has tried and failed before. He doesn't yet understand that women are more knowledgeable about seduction than young men and, once the pathway is set, they will control the pace and outcome.

Both are now lying in the tall grass and continue to talk amiably, looking at the cloudless sky and the occasional spastic fluttering of butterflies.

Paul rolls over on his side to face Cindy.

"I like to cuddle and be hugged, but I'm not going to have sex with you here," Cindy says with no rise in her tone of voice.

"I like you a lot, but if you asked me out for sex, I'm afraid I will disappoint you." She continues. "My first sex will be with my husband. Not a religious thing. I do go to church with my parents on Sundays, but I don't believe in any of that stuff anymore. Not sure anyone does, but they all still go to church, small-town ritual, like playing golf."

Paul is confused by his own sense of relief, answering, "I invited you because I liked the sound of your voice on the phone."

"Honestly?" Cindy says looking sideways at him.

"Yes," he answers, "I like sex as much as the next guy, but when the time's right," he answers to save face.

Cindy rolls over and puts her arms around Paul's shoulders drawing him near to her. She kisses him on the lips. He reciprocates, holding her tightly to him and feeling a transient surge of inexplicable grief move through him. His eyes tear up briefly. He knows only that it is not sexual but rather about being held. The grief passes and, to his discomfort, he begins to respond sensually to Cindy's warmth and the easy compliance of her softer muscles. To his surprise, the woman he imagines while talking into the receiver is in his arms.

"Hold me," she whispers in his ear.

Relieved at being told what to do, he tightens his grasp on her and she edges closer to him.

"I like just being held," she says, "My parents weren't much for holding or cuddling me when I was little... all by the book."

They lie there in the sun. Paul can think of nothing to say.

"You don't have to say anything," Cindy whispers, "just relax and enjoy it."

After a few minutes in which trilling birds and the distant hum of a tractor fill the silence between them, Cindy says, "Let's head back," and relaxes her grip on Paul.

On the ride back, neither says much, though Cindy occasionally points out passing areas of interest. Paul seems distracted, acknowledging Cindy with a smile and occasional nods. He is unsure if a response can be heard over the rush of wind and the whine of the high-compression motor.

Paul is choking. Something abrasive is moving in his throat. He hears himself coughing. A nurse is removing a feeding tube from his esophagus and the pain of its movement and the itch of its absence leads to his uncontrollable and painful coughing. At first, he thinks it is someone next to him, but he understands from the pain that he himself is coughing and that he is the only patient in the room.

1970 Fall

It's early November. Paul walks out of his afternoon French class, holding another pop quiz he has failed. In it, he was asked for the twelve irregular French verbs he was to have memorized along with their conjugations. He had made a perfunctory effort the night before, falling asleep reciting them. The next morning, however, the verb definitions are gone and there's no time to return them to memory. And the conjugations unique to each elude him entirely like the wild turkeys he and Tommy used to try to catch in the corn stover when they were little.

The quiz is no surprise and Paul no longer makes an effort to hide his ignorance of the material, turning in a sheet of largely blank paper torn from his notebook with a few mnemonic stabs at three verb meanings, but with no conjugations. The only other writing on the white-lined page is his name, the class number and the teacher's "F."

The periodic tests and quizzes only affirm the ignorance he feels. The failing grades enervate his efforts to study and increasingly he looks for distractions. A random-recall collage of images from home, events, conversations, time at the Lake with Glenda, increasingly fills his time, not studying. On the few occasions when he manages to clear his mind and make a serious effort, he retains the page architecture of the textbook and even some of the words, but he can't recall the import, definition or spelling of all the words he must retain to pass a quiz. This is less true in his English Lit. class where he easily recalls the relentless guillotining in Paris and the harrowing escape of Darnay detailed in *A Tale of Two Cities*.

Paul's adviser has twice called him in to discuss his academic status, but now seems resigned to let things take their course. Paul will not be invited back next year.

Paul leaves the Language Arts Building and walks to the student lounge to get a cup of tea. He has inherited his mother's preference for Red Rose tea over coffee, but the array of herbal teas confounds him as he searches tea bags to find a plain black tea.

Paul welcomes distractions and the wall-size bulletin board at the entrance to the cafeteria always draws his attention. He pauses to peruse the pieces of paper torn from notebooks and tacked to the off-white Homosote. Most are for buying and selling, and contain descriptive hyperbole or seek rides to and from hometowns. Others are personal, looking to replace the lost comfort of earlier friends. These notices are curiously revelatory and Paul often fantasizes about their authors. Some are coy.

"Seeking a study partner for biology, must be interested in animals. I am a dog lover and you?" followed by a dorm phone extension number. Others are more overt and surprise him with their candor.

"Are you lonely here? Me, too. Call and let's talk over coffee."

Once after checking to see that he was unseen, he pinned a note on the board with no contact information, saying simply, "Ride Wanted... to anywhere."

On this day, Paul's eye is caught by an ad, "Motorcycle for sale, 500cc '66 BSA runs ok, needs some parts. $90 as is, call Jimmy."

Paul stuffs the notice in his pockets and enters the cafeteria, where he helps himself to a cup of tea and settles into a corner table to re-read the notice.

Someone is speaking to him again, this time in the censorious voice of a school-marm. He learns that his mother is coming again to visit him that afternoon and that he should "wake up and fly right." He presumes from this that she has been here before.

It's early December and Paul and Danny are riding through the Ohio countryside, Paul on his BSA 500cc one-lunger that is, for now, running and Danny on his Vincent Black Shadow. Paul is surprised by the casual friendship to which he and his roommate have become resigned. They enjoy riding together through the Ohio cornfields when the weather is warm. It's sunny but cooler and the two ride side-by-side on a narrow, cracked-pavement farm road between two seemingly endless fields of frost-dried corn. There is no traffic, except the occasional slow-moving tractor hauling silage. It is late corn, eight feet high with tufts of pale yellow corn silk blooming from the heavy cobs. The bottom sheaves are browning out. Paul knows from his own farm that the kernels in this cow corn are small and white, more like rows of baby teeth than the kernels inside the deep yellow sugar corn that his mother grows at one end of her garden. Her "table corn" as she calls it grows next to the rhubarb patch and the pile of dried manure that Leon keeps nearby for her.

Paul has never seen Italians, at least that he is aware of, so he does not identify his black-haired roommate as such. Danny is shorter than Paul, who has now reached his mature height of six feet. Danny's hair is neatly trimmed above the ears, as his family and friends back home are disdainful of the emerging hippy culture they see in Time magazine with its emblematic long hair. Plus, Danny's cousin Lenny gives him free haircuts every two or three weeks. Paul is unaware of his hair altogether and thus untroubled by its length. Besides, he can ill afford to spend money to have someone cut it.

Danny is plagued with what Paul hears called "zits." He has noticed a few friends back home develop acne, but nothing like the red and purple welts that plague his roommate's oily skin. Neither did Paul know that acne could occur other than on one's face. Danny's back and neck are knotty with welts similar to those on his face. Danny washes his face several times a day with soap from a pale green bottle that he tells Paul surgeons use to wash their hands before operating on someone. This is all new to Paul who feels sympathy for his roommate's bad skin.

Paul and Danny are in search of a bar they've been told sells beers for a quarter and half-gallon pitchers for a buck. It's not a student bar, though some students from nearby have found it. It's a venue for local farmers on weeknights and for farmers and their wives on Saturday nights. It's closed Sundays. There's a local hillbilly band that performs high tenor duets by the Bolick Brothers and a swing band that plays Bob Wills' tunes. The bands alternate Saturday nights, playing for an overflow crowd of farmers and hired hands. College boys are tolerated but not welcome. The few who show up are shown the door if they get rowdy, though that is not the case with the farmers.

Danny's bike is capable of racetrack speeds, while Paul's is a constant source of mechanical anxiety, burning oil and stalling while idling. The chain tensioner is broken so the chain is always loose. The clutch cable is corroded and shifting requires manual finesse, whereas Danny's bike requires no thought, only caution. Its 1,000 cc V-twin hangs comfortably in its alloy frame, making it a rocket.

They ride through a succession of gently rolling hills of corn basking in the low autumn sun. There are no road signs on the rare intersections, so Paul keeps the sun's position in mind. The familiar mountain peaks with which he orients himself at home do not exist in this part of Ohio. Danny is stoned.

A friend has told them where the bar is, but they've been riding for an hour and haven't found it and it's supposed to be only twenty-five minutes from campus.

Danny is also impatient and he occasionally wearies of staying abreast of Paul and races ahead half a mile, slowing then to wait for Paul to catch up. They stop and Paul tweaks the throttle cable going from the right hand control to the carburetor. This gives a bit more high-end. He wishes he'd had enough money for the used Ducati, but it was three times as much as the BSA.

They take off again. Danny shoots ahead over the next hill and Paul crests the hill not far behind him. Near the bottom of the hill, Danny stops now on the narrow shoulder. He dismounts the idling bike and clamps his right hand to his ear. There is blood running profusely through his fingers. Ohio has no helmet laws yet. Paul is confused. Danny has not fallen off. The bike is upright. Danny lowers the kickstand with his right boot.

Paul pulls up behind him and kills his bike reluctantly as it is always hard to start and they're in the middle of nowhere. He is appalled by the flow of blood. Danny takes his hand away so Paul can see what happened. Half of Danny's ear hangs from a sliver of cartilage. Neither understands what has just caused this injury.

Paul rips Danny a bandana from his T-shirt to staunch the flow of blood and to keep the piece of ear intact. They agree to race back to the infirmary, even as they both understand that the wound is not life-threatening. Danny jumps on the idling Vincent. Paul jumps on the BSA, cranks it once slowly, and then jumps on the starter. After eight tries, they decide to hide the bike in the cornfield and take the Vincent. Paul pushes the bike with some difficulty through several furrows and lays it down where it can't be seen from the road. He lays a rock on the remains of his t-shirt to remind him where his bike is. He climbs on the Vincent behind Danny. Danny pops the shift lever down with his left boot and releases the clutch while accelerating. The motor races but the bike goes nowhere. Danny looks down. There is no chain between the drive wheel and the rear axle.

He kills the Vincent. It becomes clear to both riders what happened.

"I must've thrown the chain when I down-shifted coming down the hill," Danny says. "Now we'll have to get your clunker started. It will start, won't it?"

"Eventually," answers Paul heading back into the corn. "Ain't gonna be easy getting that Vincent, light as it is, hidden back in there." He emerges from the corn pushing the BSA and the two manage to push the 500-pound Vincent far enough in to be out of sight. Paul tries to start his bike, while Danny walks back up the hill to see if he can find the chain.

A passing pickup with a German shepherd in the back slows and the driver asks, "You boys OK? Ya need a hand?"

"Bike threw a chain. Thanks, we'll be OK."

"Give ya a lift if ya want. Goin' ta Bowlin' Green. Say, what happened ta your head? You sure you're OK?

"Yeah. Just a surface injury, more blood than hurt. I'm OK," Danny yells back. He has inherited from his clandestine father an intrinsic suspicion of even well-meaning strangers.

Just as the truck drives off, the BSA fires and the two pass the truck. They reach the infirmary in less than an hour.

That night with a flashlight, the two leave in the GTO with the trailer to retrace their steps and recover the Vincent. Danny drives with 64 milligrams of codeine in his circulatory system from the minor surgery, his airways and sinuses are flush with hashish, and he grips an Iron City in his right hand.

Paul, who doesn't share his roommate's penchant for psychotropic drugs, navigates with only an Iron City from the six-pack between them and his memory of the day's earlier ride.

Paul hears a familiar voice and opens his eyes. His mother's hands are covering her face. "Nurse, I think he's coming out of the coma," she says fearfully. The nurse joins his mother at the bedside. Paul blinks into the pale light of an unfamiliar room.

"Well, hello, there, stranger," the nurse says cheerfully. "So you finally decided to join us again. Nice to have you back. Say 'hello' to your mother."

Paul cannot speak, but his mother knows she has been acknowledged by her son.

The following Friday, Danny alerts Paul that he has a date with a girl he met in history class, saying only that she has red hair and admires his Vincent. Paul hears this news as conversational, not catching the premonitory tone in his roommate's voice. Paul then decides to ask Cindy out again.

Paul has been thinking of Cindy and decides to ask her out again. She made clear when saying goodbye on their first date that she doesn't see boys during the week, thus avoiding questions from her parents about whom she is seeing.

Still unfamiliar with what the campus offers socially that a "townie" might enjoy other than rowdy weekend keg and speed parties migrating from frat house to frat house, Paul asks Cindy what she would like to do. She suggests he show her around the campus and then share a bottle of Chianti, which it turns out she is old enough to order, and some pasta at a local Italian eatery that her family frequents.

Grateful not to have to research options and make a decision, Paul agrees. After dinner, they go back to his dorm room and, as predicted, find Danny out.

They talk comfortably about school. Cindy is curious and asks Paul many questions about what it's like to be in college, what he learns in his classes, how much he has to study, how much reading he must do, and if rote memorization is still part of the learning she remembers struggling with in high school.

Paul cannot answer all her questions about homework, as he now does little of it, and spends much of his time in class daydreaming of home and the practical things he has spent most of his life doing. He wants only to begin the next phase of his life, on which his few friends at home have embarked: getting jobs, earning money, and maintaining cars and farm equipment using familiar tools.

Cindy again initiates a demure and experimental intimacy with Paul as the two settle back on his single cot. She places Paul's right hand on her left breast, moaning softly as his hand conforms to the soft tissue barely filling the wired cup beneath her blouse. This is only his second or third time touching the breast of a young woman and he, too, is aroused. He moves his hand slowly down toward her waist, but she returns his hand to her breast and encourages his gentle fondling above her waist.

In the pale light Paul looks closely at the woman in his arms. He is enthralled at the sensuous access she affords him, but feels oddly distanced from her as a person, almost as if she is trying him out for a role in her life.

She leaves around 10:30, citing a promise to help her mother the following day.

Paul finds himself aroused and alone. He doesn't know whether he misses Cindy or the stimulus of her proximity.

Soon he falls asleep in the disorder of his bed. Sometime in the middle of the night, he is awakened by sustained and noisy movement in the cot parallel to his own. He opens his eyes into the pale light of an exterior street light to see Danny on top of a woman. Paul again sees the minefield of minor infections on the nape of his roommate's neck and back. Danny and his date are in the throes of sex. Paul has never seen this before, though he has imagined it many times. He remains perfectly still, pretending to be asleep but watching his roommate's accelerating fervor, and trying to fathom the physiology. He has nothing to relate it to except his own occasional masturbation. His roommate gasps and rolls off his date, who, once in full view, seems to be asleep already and the room is suddenly silent.

Paul lies wide awake in the bluish aura of the streetlight, trying to replay what he has seen that might help him when his own time comes but learns only that the rule about women leaving the dorms by 10 p.m. is either unenforced or ignored.

Discomfited by the clinical frenzy he's witnessed, he soon falls asleep in the half-light. Danny's sleep, however, is agitated as he tries repeatedly to get comfortable next to the inert body taking up most of his cot.

In the morning Paul tries to sneak out before Danny and his date wake up so they will not be embarrassed by his presence the night before. As he pulls on his jeans, a feminine voice says, "Good morning. Sorry about last night. It was either my roommate or Danny's and he said you'd be cool. Hope we didn't keep you awake."

"No, I sleep soundly," he says.

Paul feels the cool touch of his mother's hand on his own. It is an unfamiliar touch. The calloused and muscled hand he remembers feels now more like a cool membrane stretched over a frail geology of arteries and tendons. He can feel the bones in her hand. How, he wonders, have these hands changed so much? Perhaps his mother is much older than he remembers. He has lost any sense of elapsed time and tries to recall how long it has been since he has seen her. He doesn't know how long he's been asleep or, for that matter, that he has been asleep or where he is.

He hears his mother talking to him. He can see her lips moving and hears a voice, but the two are out of synch, and he is distracted by this and misses her words.

"Later," he hears her say, "I'll come back later. Get some rest."

"How is father?" he believes he asks, but doesn't.

1977 Spring

Paul's relationship with Danny has become practical as Paul has no money and Danny does. Paul sees that Danny knows this and often feels like he is becoming a houseboy to his roommate. Danny has regaled Paul with stories about the domestics in their suburban Chicago home. He describes them as servants when and jokes about their foibles and their alien patter, making clear that his parents and siblings expect little more of them than to do their bidding. Danny's condescending stories of their mistakes and mishaps make Paul uncomfortable as he has no experience with being waited on.

Tommy's mother, Norma, once cleaned house every week for the manager of the bank that now owns their home, but always said she was treated like a member of the family during her employment. When Paul asks Danny if the servants live with his family, Danny laughs and says, "Christ, no! There's no blacks allowed in our neighborhood except to work." When Paul asks where they do live, Danny professes to have no idea.

Danny's been drinking all day and has missed his afternoon classes. He appears to be maintaining a desired equilibrium between beer and the Dexedrine his father mails him ostensibly for all-night study sessions. This state of high-energy inebriation is Danny's favorite place to be.

An ad hoc party is developing on the dorm patio downstairs. Someone has hauled stereo components down into the common space and the French doors have been thrown open onto the patio where drunken heads bob to the Motown music blaring from two bookshelf speakers set up on the patio floor. Two couples are dancing to a tune by the Temptations.

Danny decides that rum punch is in order and suggests that Paul run into town and get a half -gallon of rum and some canned juice. Danny does not offer to let him take his car. It's dusk and the headlight on Paul's bike has stopped working. One of the loose wires going into the rusty chrome headlight housing is unattached inside the fixture and Paul has yet to disassemble it and resolder it onto the bulb socket. The light periodically springs to life and then dies again.

Danny offers Paul a deal he can't refuse, handing him two twenties and telling him to keep the change. Paul pulls on his backpack, as he has no saddle bags on his bike, and quietly leaves. The liquor store that sells to minors is in the next town and the trip is about 20 minutes each way.

Paul feels the weight of a half gallon of rum in a glass bottle and three quart cans of Caribbean Punch in his backpack. He is going faster coming home than he did going there as clouds have obscured the moon somewhat and he can only see the outline of the tarmac ahead of him. No center or shoulder lines are painted on the frost-heaved road.

He is traveling under a canopy of dying elms and has had to slow down somewhat when suddenly he feels a massive impact against his chest, as if he has been hit by a falling tree branch. He downshifts abruptly while trying to catch his breath. It is not clear what has hit him. He downshifts again, releasing the clutch and brings his left hand to his chest where he feels the sticky warmth of fresh blood. He brakes hard now and pulls over to the side of the road where he pulls off his backpack and drops down on the shoulder to recover his breath. He is covered with blood and soon realizes, with feathers.

When he catches his breath and is again on his feet, he realizes he has hit a large bird and that it knocked the wind out of him. He walks back a few yards and a barn owl is lying in a pool of blood in the middle of the road. It must have hit the headlight or bars first as it seems torn in two.

The moon emerges from behind a cloud and Paul grabs his backpack, remounts the idling bike and speeds back to the dorm in the waning moonlight.

Danny looks him over with a smirk and asks, "What happened to you? You're covered with feathers. They tar and feather you? I know they don't like hippies. Looks like you tried to fly home! That junker fail you again? What a mess! I wouldn't come down stairs looking like that. You might ruin the party mood. Go change and come on down; should be fun." With that, he relieves Paul of his backpack and descends to the swelling party on the first floor to mix punch.

Feeling like the scolded servant he has become, Paul returns to their room and slides his wallet, now enriched with $18.35, into his pillowcase and walks to the empty men's room where he enters the row of open showers fully clothed. He removes first his shirt and then his jeans, holding them under the shower flow until all the feathers and blood are washed away. Finally, he removes the mass of downy feathers from the shower's drain grate and throws the wet mass into the wastebasket at the end of a line of sinks. He splashes his face, arms and hands with cold water, returns to his room in his underwear, and gets into bed. He lies there for an hour thinking of Glenda and home before finally falling asleep.

Paul suddenly experiences searing pain. With one eye open and flashing in panic he sees his leg in traction. He tries to thrash but is immobilized by aluminum braces lined with putty-colored Ace bandage material. He makes some guttural noises with the sputum deep in his throat. The recovery nurse hears him and approaches.

"Where do you hurt?" she asks, "Where? Can you tell me where it hurts?"

Paul tries to move his head, but the entreaty in his eyes is more fluent.

The nurse looks away at the IV bottle, leaves, and returns with a full one for an exchange. She adjusts a blue knurled valve in the clear vinyl tubing, checks the IV line's entry into the fold of his elbow and says, "This'll make you feel better," and leaves. Paul looks in terror at her retreating back.

In less than a minute, the waves of pain subside and he is floating on his back in the still water of Long Pond. He knows Glenda is on the shore sunbathing and watching him. The temperature of the pond is the same as the temperature of his body and his sensory deprivation is breached only by the brilliant sun shining down on him. The pond is like glass.

Paul and Cindy make another date during which Paul comes to understand that his infatuation with her has not grown beyond the sound of her voice, the warm exploration of her soft flesh, and the languorous pain of unconsummated sex. She is sweet to him. She is clear and honest with him about what she wants and what she will or will not trade for it., but Paul does not know these things about himself yet and can't barter.

When he is with her, he thinks of Glenda and wonders how she is, what Montreal is like and if there are places to swim. He remembers as a child crossing the Champlain Bridge over the St. Lawrence River into Montreal, seeing the giant ore ships leaving the Great Lakes. He remembers, and looking out the window of his father's car at the massive concrete grain silos that would have held a thousand times the silage in their own wood-slat silo, and finally entering. Then they would enter the forest of downtown skyscrapers.

They were on their way to a family reunion in Mont Royal Park on the mountain above Sherbrooke Street. Often, these are the things he thinks about when he is with Cindy. She knows he is far away when she talks to him and he will never be there in the way she needs him to be, though they both seem to enjoy the physical intimacy and throttled urgency of desire they incite in one another. It is not enough, however, and Cindy does not call Paul and Paul does not think to call her again.

More often now, he rides his motorcycle through the nearby countryside alone, though he can never be sure of what will happen mechanically. If he does break down, there is no one to call except Danny, but on the rare occasions when he's in their dorm room, Danny is stoned and doesn't like to answer the phone.

Paul has just left a meeting with his adviser who has begun dropping hints that Paul will not be invited back because of his academic performance. Paul is aware that his adviser is mincing words to spare him embarrassment.

Paul listens, asking only that it be left to him to tell his parents. He is assured that the school will not send a formal notice of dismissal to his home. His semester's grades will be sent home as a matter of course and they will say what no formal letter would convey.

Paul leaves that night, saying goodbye to Danny, who palms him some twenty dollar bills and wishes him luck. Paul takes none of his things except a gym bag of clothing. He asks Danny to throw the rest out.

The next day, Paul hears voices and tries to open an eye. But his eyelid seems glued shut. He is groggy. It takes several seconds to open his one eye and bring it into focus. He scans the seven people at his bedside without moving his head. He recognizes no one.

"Do you know where you are?" he hears a male voice ask. "Paul, can you answer me?" the voice asks again.

Paul's monocular stare rescans the group, looking for someone he knows.

The voice resumes, "You're in the trauma center ICU. You were moved here last night by ambulance. You had a bad motorcycle accident. We'll need your help in your recovery. You'll be all right, but only if you help us. It will take a lot of work on both our parts, but you are going to live."

The voices by his bedstead continue to talk among themselves. They refer to him in the third person as if he were not there. He hears them, but not what they are saying. He wonders again if his bike is okay and where it is.

Paul is outside the city limits driving west through the countryside. He has no destination. He is *leaving* somewhere, but not necessarily *going* anywhere. He rides through several Ohio farm towns. He has looped the back of his belt through the handles of his gym bag behind him and it occasionally shifts sides as he leans into a curve.

It will soon be dark and he will need to find a place to stay. He wishes he could call and talk with Glenda. He has her number in his wallet, but the complexity of calling a foreign country from a coin phone somewhere in the Midwest and the idea of a telephone ring echoing down an empty corridor in a dorm in Montreal waiting for someone to answer dissuades him from calling. The two times he has gotten through to her, the phone was first answered in French by a stranger. He repeated Glenda's name and room number and poured more coins into the chrome slot in the phone before he heard her voice.

In the periphery of his headlight's glow, he sees a hand-painted sign on the porch of a well-kept house that says, "Guests." He rolls back the throttle and downshifts until he rolls to a stop just ahead of the house. He rolls the idling bike back several yards with his heels and turns the handlebars toward the unlit porch to aim the headlight on the sign. He drops the kickstand, switches off the bike by pulling apart the twisted ignition wires in front of the gas tank, removes his gym bag from his belt, and walks up onto the porch. At the sound of steps, a light comes on and the door opens. An elderly woman asks if she can help him while she looks him up and down.

"I'm wondering if I could get a room for a night. How much is it?" he asks politely.

The woman is still assessing him. She looks over her shoulder at the motorcycle by the front gate and answers, "$7.50 a night. How long would you be staying with us? It's cheaper by the week or month, of course."

"I think just for tonight," he answers.

"Would you like to see the room?" she continues.

"I'm sure it will be lovely," he smiles, setting her farther at ease. ""I'll take it if you'll have me."

"Of course," she responds, "Breakfast is included."

She is pleased to find such a well-brought-up young man. Sometimes she lies, saying that she is full when she sees unsavory young men on motorcycles or hot rods pull up.

Paul wipes his feet on the doormat and follows her up the stairs to a sparse, clean bedroom with a comfortable looking iron-frame bed and a dark oak-veneer dresser. The bed reminds him of his and Glenda's room at home except it is nicely painted and has a full ceiling.

"I only take single working men and women usually, as I have no larger beds, traveling salesmen for the most part. I have a few regulars," she continues amiably. "The bath is down the hall and there's a glass and clean towels in your room. I usually ask that people pay up front."

"Paul extracts one of the twenties that Danny gave him from his wallet and gives it to her. I'll get you change she says.

"It's OK," he responds smiling, "I'll get it at breakfast." She, too, smiles, pleased that her trust is reciprocated.

Paul falls asleep thinking of his Uncle Theron, wondering how he is faring. He knows that Theron's increasingly eccentric behavior is a source of worry for his mother.

He lies down on the bed and the chemistry of sleep overtakes his thoughts. He dreams in intricate detail about the paths and clearings that Theron maintains around his cabin, the corduroy road leading to the brook and the stand of small cedars on the other side where they once saw a small black bear rummaging for grubs.

For the first time in many months, Paul sleeps soundly between clean, ironed sheets. He awakes refreshed, remembering none of his dreams. Nor is he anxious about going to another class unprepared and at a loss for excuses, which he had eventually abandoned in favor of stony silence.

He smells toast. He goes into the bathroom, combs his hair and throws cold water on his face, then gets dressed and goes down to breakfast.

Mrs. Benton is already seated at the table and greets him, asking if he is a coffee or tea drinker and whether he likes strawberry- rhubarb jam or honey on his toast. Paul asks for tea with milk and allows that the jam sounds delicious.

"I made it myself. Over easy or scrambled?" she continues, bustling up from her chair and taking a departing sip of her tea.

"Can I be of any help?" Paul inquires.

"You just have a seat," Mrs. Benton says. That sign says "guest" and you're my guest. I'll be right out with your breakfast ... growing boys need a good breakfast."

"Thank you, ma'am," Paul answers.

He is not used to being cared for since he left home.

Shortly, Mrs. Benton returns with a pale blue china plate with buttered toast, a mound of scrambled eggs, and a rasher of bacon.

"I have some apple juice if you'd like," she adds.

"This'll be fine," he smiles, "more than I usually eat. Thank you."

Mrs. Benton sits back down and again sips her milky tea

"What brings you to our town? Or you just passing through?" she asks.

"Headed west a bit to find some work and see some more country. Not sure my ride will get me much farther though. It's not in very good shape. Probably have to find some work around here before I travel much more. Have you lived here long?"

"I moved here with my husband after he came back from the War. He was in the Pacific, you know. Let me tell you, those guys had it hard. George was a good man, haunted by what he saw there. He was a flame thrower operator in the occupied islands off Japan, used to wake up at night sobbing. Good man. Worked at the Chrysler plant in Toledo. Had his first heart attack at 46, then the big one two years later. I still miss him every day. I make do with his small pension, Social Security, and my occasional guests. Still sleep on the same side of the bed I used to when he was with me. He was a big man and the mattress still bears his impression. Sometimes in my dreams, I reach out to see if he's there. Silly ... don't know why I'm telling you all this." She looks off out the bay window in her dining room, still holding her teacup in midair.

"I bet he was a fine man. Sorry you lost him so young," Paul says quietly.

Paul eats in silence, giving Mrs. Benton a chance to recover.

She turns to him with an appreciative smile and asks, "Where do you hail from?"

"Northern Vermont," Paul answers with a mouthful of eggs and toast. He chews for a minute and then continues, "Middle of nowhere really; nice country, but pretty wild, not much to do there except farming and hunting."

"Do your folks still live there?" inquires Mrs. Benton.

"Yes, they still farm. Gets hard as you get older, especially with my sister and me away. I plan to go home, probably in the fall, and help out."

"What brought you here? Hope I'm not being too nosy," Mrs. Benton giggles.

"I tried a year of college at Bowling Green, but it wasn't for me, at least not now," Paul answers, feeling sheepish.

"College isn't for everybody. Neither George nor I ever went to college, and we made do just fine. He used to read all the time. Loved books about the Civil War. Bookshelf in our bedroom is filled with his books about that war. Funny, he didn't seem interested in his own war, probably too close. His prized possession was an autographed copy of *Andersonville*. MacKinlay Kantor, the author, was speaking in Toledo and George went there to hear him and ask him to sign his copy. He prized that book. I never read it. I knew from the pictures that it would be too sad. I have to work to keep a happy mind. I think the book reminded him of his time in Borneo."

Paul helps Mrs. Benton clear the table over her protests. She is a heavyset woman; not fat, but with the gentle weight of advancing years and homemade pastries. Her light brown skin hangs loosely on her facial bones and her smiling face has the soft wrinkles and wattles that endow her age. The backs of her hands are dotted with liver spots and white hair shows faint blue traces of the rinse her hairdresser uses once a month.

"If you do any carpentry, they're building 28 houses twelve miles down the road. My friend Tilda's husband is the surveyor there. I know they're hiring on if you don't mind pounding nails and hauling lumber," Mrs. Benton offers.

"Can I come back another night? I think I'll go see if they'll take me on. I've done framing, but never finish work. I could use some more travel cash and will need a more dependable ride. Hasn't rained since I left, but I'm not looking forward to riding this thing in the rain. Barely runs as it is."

"You get here before 5:30 and you can share my supper. Making George's favorite, a beef stew, and none of that canned stuff, either."

Paul makes his bed and leaves his gym bag by the dresser.

"I'll be back. Thanks for having me," he says with a smile as he closes the front door.

He twists the ignition wires together and closes the choke. He has come to know the kick pattern for his bike, though it rarely works until several tries, after which the carburetor floods and he has to wait and start the whole sequence again. He gently pumps the kick start until he feels the full compression of the engine. He waits for a second and then jumps on the crank. He hears the fire, but it doesn't catch. After several repetitions, the engine fires and sputters to life, emitting a dense blue smoke from the rusty chrome pipe. He throttles back to reduce the noise and burn off moisture. When the cylinder head is warm to the touch, he engages the clutch and pops the bike into first, driving off quietly, and only opening the throttle far enough down the road so that his departure doesn't signal anything untoward to Mrs. Benton.

Paul is becoming increasingly conscious and aware of his surroundings. With his one eye he records the sequence of events in intensive care, both for himself and the two other patients with whom he now shares the unit. He watches catheter bags being emptied, bed pillows fluffed and patients turned in their beds, feeding tubes removed, IVs replaced, and periodic injections. The dimly lit room is silent except for the hum and respiration of a ventilator.

He knows he'll soon have to respond to the rounds of doctors and nurses who arrive to question him and to the daily visits by his mother. He wonders what city he is in and how far his parents must travel to see him.

Up to now, the only thing over which he has had any control is whether or not to answer the myriad questions asked of him. He is not sure if his voice works at all and begins to practice when he wakes up and there is no one around. With no night or day, no identifiable meals, and no visible clock, he remains disoriented. Nor does he know what season it is outside. When he is alone, he pretends that Glenda is with him and talks to her. The words coming out of his mouth are whispered and somewhat raspy but comprehensible, and he is increasingly confident that he has both the vocal and mental capacity to answer the questions he has been ignoring for several days.

It's been three weeks. He likes the people on the jobsite. To his surprise, he was hired in spite of his honesty about having no experience in construction. He's assigned as a rodman to work with a surveyor named Freddy. Freddy graduated from the local community college with a degree in civil engineering and has finished laying out the 28 house sites to be built on this 18-acre field, now flensed of topsoil. Paul and Freddy work with an excavator operator named Jerry, laying out and digging cellar holes, one and a half in a day. Jerry runs the digger, Freddy, the transit, and Paul walks around to various points in the cellar hole holding upright and more or less level the 16-foot rod with its white enamel background and black elevation numbers. Their work is not always line-of-sight and Paul is often hoarse by day's end, trying to yell over the roar of Jerry's excavator digging in the same hole.

When Paul returns to the jobsite each morning at seven, he first peers into the finished hole from the day before to watch men erecting wooden concrete forms. Elsewhere on the site several drivers chat while their diesel cement trucks idle nearby, tumbling the wet slurry that will become the walls of workshops, mother-in-law rooms, or family playrooms.

Paul is surprised at the pay and concludes that laborers make more money in Ohio than they do in Vermont. The $3.20 an hour he makes is a dollar more than he would expect to earn at home. Mrs. Benton has extended him her "long-stay" rate of $55 monthly with no obligation on his part, so Paul is able to save almost $50 a week after gas and the meatloaf sandwich and chocolate milk he buys from the snack truck every day at 11:30. He is used to riding his bike in the rain and has grown more accustomed to dealing with the anomalies of the quirky British bike. Mrs. Benton directs him to a mechanic she says "can fix anything from a mangle to a Cadillac Seville."

Paul spends $114 on parts and labor and has all the original control cables and the headlight and ignition switches on the bike replaced, though the switches are U.S. Army surplus toggle switches, jury-rigged to the right handle bar. As a bonus, the mechanic tunes the carburetor, which boosts Paul's confidence in the cranky machine and makes it easier to start.

Paul's only other expense is an occasional call to Glenda. During noon break, he inhales his sandwich, leaving enough time to ride to the bank in town to get a roll of quarters for the coin phone a half mile from Mrs. Benton's. He doesn't know how to get "time and charges" from the operator and also doesn't want to importune Mrs. Benton by using her phone.

It's an extravagance he wishes to keep to himself, especially since one of Glenda's dorm mates answers the phone, disappears to find her and often picks up the receiver again several minutes later to announce that she can't find her in her room or in the lounge. Paul asks only that the girl leave word with Glenda that he is all right and that he will try again, knowing it is pointless to leave the number of a glass phone booth at the intersection of two rural roads in the middle of Ohio.

One night, he dreams that the phone is ringing as he rides by. He stops his bike and runs to grab the receiver before Glenda hangs up. He grabs the receiver from its cradle but the voice that answered is that of a gruff and impatient man looking for someone named "Ellie." He wakes up agitated by the dream and the pall of isolation it leaves over him. Lying on his side, he looks out at the field bathed in the silver light of a waxing moon.

He knows not to call home, as his parents would expect a long-distance call to bring only bad news. He writes several letters to his parents with formal vellum stationery he borrows from Mrs. Benton, saying only that he is okay and that he is in the Midwest working. He does not address the issue of his leaving college before the end of the year. He promises to stay in touch and that he will be home after he has made some more money. He puts in a few sentences about the nature of his job that he thinks might be of interest to his father and that, if nothing else, might signal his industry and self-reliance, but his words don't fill a whole sheet of Mrs. Benton's stationery before he signs off, licks the acrid glue, and presses the flap tight against its envelope. Mrs. Benton always gives him an approving smile at breakfast when he shows up with one of her envelopes and asks her to add it to her outgoing mail, though he knows she never has any.

A month passes before he again tries Glenda. Several weeks of hazy, overcast days have finally broken out into torrents of rain that last five days, slowing work at the site. The water puddling in the cellar holes soon becomes so deep that transit elevations are impossible to measure, as the red clay turns into a slurry of mud. Jerry tries with his excavator to ladle the mire out of the holes, but the mounds soon wash back into the cellar holes. The crew trying to set concrete forms finally quits, committing to return when the jobsite dries up.

Paul leaves work at 4:30. The crew boss lets him keep his bike in the cover of a small lean-to erected to keep carpenters' tool belts and power tools dry. He walks his bike to the paved road, starts it, and drives straight to the phone booth.

After a long wait that consumes three quarters, he finally hears Glenda's voice and senses that something is amiss.

"Uncle Theron died," she says before her customary questions about his well-being.

"Dad found him at his cabin when he hiked in to bring him some groceries and a meat pie mom had made."

He hears several abrupt sniffles as she collects herself.

"What happened?" he asks.

"Dad didn't know," Glenda answers still sniffling.

"Dad said he found him lying in his cot as if he were at a wake. It was uncanny as dad described it... almost as if Uncle Theron had laid himself out to die. He was on his back; only his eyes were open. There was a short note, but dad didn't say what was in it."

"Did he kill himself?" Paul asks.

"Not that dad said. He would have told us if he had, but dad said he looked perfectly calm and there were no injuries on his body. Only thing different than if he were in a casket, dad said was his eyes were open."

Paul is silent now. He can see his uncle exactly as his father had described him to Glenda.

"You've got to call home, Paul. Mom and dad are worried sick about you. They get your letters, but they don't know why you left college, where you are or even if you're okay. They only know you're alive and working somewhere. Please call them tonight."

"I will, I promise," answers Paul half-heartedly.

"When did Uncle Theron die?" Paul continues.

"I don't know what day, but dad found him late Saturday morning. All he could say was that he looked peaceful."

"And he didn't say what was in the note?" Paul persists

"No, but if you call, I'm sure dad will tell you. After all, Uncle Theron was dad's brother, Paul. Promise me you'll call tonight," Glenda urges.

"I can't call now, I don't have enough coins, but I promise I'll call tomorrow as soon as I get out of work," Paul says, believing himself.

The conversation winds up with Paul's telling Glenda that he wishes Montreal were closer to where he is.

Paul has only seven quarters left from the roll he bought at the bank last month. He puts the roll back in his pocket and leaves the booth, closing the folding door behind him. He is caught off guard when he hears the phone start ringing inside the booth, as if his closing the door had somehow triggered the ring. He worries for a second that it is the operator calling him back to ask him to deposit more money. As he opens the door, it occurs to him that he has not heard a phone ring since the day he was hired. The phone in the construction trailer on the desk of the construction boss who had just hired him rang as he left the trailer. He has never heard Mrs. Benton's phone ring.

"Hello," he answers tentatively.

"How are you?" he hears a female voice say. He doesn't recognize the voice.

"It's me, Cindy. I'm really sorry about your uncle. I really am. Are you OK? Were you close?" she asks.

"Cindy?" he asks confused. "How did you know? Were you listening?" Paul asks, still nonplussed by the toll phone's ring.

"I sometimes connect your calls. There are only eight of us girls in this CO and sometimes I hear you calling Glenda in Montreal. I never listen in, but I did this time, I'm sorry. I didn't know she was family. I thought maybe she was your girlfriend. I'd be fired if anyone knew I listened in. I am so sorry about your uncle."

Assimilating the sequential logic of what has just happened, Paul remembers that Cindy is an operator, must have connected his call to Glenda, would know the phone booth's number, has called him back in the phone booth, and has listened in on his call. Grateful to hear the familiar voice, he recalls the few times when he and Cindy simply held one another without needing to talk. In spite of the whiplash sequence of events, he answers her, even as he can see his uncle lying dead in his cot.

Cindy's whispered tone indicates that she is taking a risk by talking to him. The call ends abruptly when she whispers, "I've got to go."

Paul holds the receiver away and looks out through the steady rain and fading light, still hearing the urgency in Glenda's voice, the news of Theron's death, and the sound and memory of Cindy's voice and touch.

When he returns to Mrs. Benton's, the house is redolent with the smell of pot roast. He has forgotten his hunger. At work, he decided to forgo spending four of his telephone quarters for lunch and bought a cup of milky coffee instead while grabbing a handful of free soup crackers from the sandwich truck.

Mrs. Benton trills her usual "Have a good day?" as she places a steaming plate of stew before him. A surge of unexpected gratitude wells up in his throat for her kindness and throttles his response. "Good enough, except the rain's made a mess of everything. Much harder to work with mud," he adds, smiling up at her. "How was your day?"

"Much the same, much the same," she says pulling her chair out from the table and sitting down.

He decides not to break the comity of their evening together by relaying the news of his uncle's death. It can wait, and he needs time to frame the words he will use to tell her about his uncle, and to set his demeanor in telling such news. Is it best to be sad or matter-of-fact?

He dreams that night of his Uncle Theron's cabin, though not of Theron himself. Paul is there alone, though it seems that his uncle is just around the corner everywhere he goes.

Paul is again surrounded by strangers who, for lack of any response to their repetitive questions, shuffle off after briefly reviewing Paul's chart and discussing upcoming surgeries. The next surgery will be the most difficult, he overhears, and the first of at least three. He learns that first, however, they will administer nerve conduction studies to assess the extent of his spinal cord injury and that he will be conscious. They cannot proceed, however, until he is responsive and is able to answer questions about what he feels and where.

Glenda stays behind. She has been to visit him several times before. The hospital to which he has been transferred is only an hour and a half from Montreal and she takes the bus.

Unsure of his voice or of what to say, he hasn't responded to her presence until now.

"Hi, Sis," he whispers.

Glenda's face lights up and she approaches his bedside, takes his one free hand and asks, "How do you feel? Are you OK? Does it hurt? I'm so glad you're alive. What happened, for Christ's sake? There was no other car."

"Coon," he rasps, "Goddamn raccoon in the road."

"Someone said that might be the case. Dad said, when the police went back, they said there was a road-kill near the accident. Did you hit it?"

"Dead-on, biggest 'coon I've ever seen; looked like a fur-bearing igloo; sent me flying. I only remember bits and pieces of what happened, like a picture show where the film keeps breaking, remember?"

Glenda smiles at Paul.

"Let me catch them and tell them you're speaking now," Glenda says.

"Not yet, Sis, I need more time. I'm just not up to their questions yet. I know I'm badly hurt. I hear them talking about me like I'm not here, but haven't had it in me to answer them. It only hurts when they move me. How long have I been here?"

"The accident was nine days ago. Paul, you've got to help them. They're saying they can't fix you unless you help," she insists.

The urgency in Glenda's voice reminds him of when he called her and learned of Uncle Theron's death, and how she begged him to call home and talk to their parents. He can't remember ever hearing urgency in Glenda's voice when they were kids.

Paul's mind is struggling against a new nepenthe drip hanging in a clear glass bottle above his head. The drops entering his bloodstream through a needle taped to the crotch in his elbow wreak havoc with the time code of his memory.

The last thing he hears before falling asleep again is Glenda telling him that Theron left them the deer camp.

It's mid-October and construction is winding down. Only four cellar holes remain to be dug and leveled. When his job as rodman is over, the job foreman has promised Paul continued employment as a day laborer but at the same pay because of his solid work performance.

A week before, where Paul, Freddy and Jerry are now working, concrete forms are peeled away and reassembled in the next empty hole. Dry foundation perimeters were back-filled with gravel and then the red clay was pushed back in place by a small 'dozer and leveled, as carpenters raise 2 x 6 frames from the footings. Two weeks farther back, plumbers and electricians tunneled through joists and floors, installing the residential intestines and central nervous system of the look-alike houses. A month back, men framed, sheathed, and shingled roofs; while below them laborers carried premade cabinets and appliances in the front door to finish carpenters inside.

When Paul looks at the cellar holes they dug in mid-July, he sees real estate sales people showing couples and families finished two- and three-bedroom houses at the far end of the field in which they have been working. The recently sodded lawns retain their tiled look. The uniform foundation plantings and wire-supported white birch clusters with mounds of bark mulch at their base have yet to make themselves at home.

Freddy invites Paul to a Veteran's Day party at the VFW in his hometown. Paul accepts. The work routine, though comforting, has become boring. He has taken to reading several of the Reader's Digest condensed editions that Mrs. Benton offered him from the bookshelf to the right of the living room fireplace. These are books he did not see in high school at home and among his favorites are *Cry, the Beloved Country* by Alan Paton, *Return to Paradise* by James Michener, *The Caine Mutiny* by Herman Wouk, *The Cruel Sea* by Nicholas Monsarrat, *At Play in the Fields of the Lord* by Peter Matthiessen, and *Kamante and Lulu* by Isak Dinesen.

On Saturdays, if Mrs. Benton doesn't have some errand or chore for him to do around the house, Paul often makes up some excuse and goes for a long ride in the countryside. He keeps a wrinkled Ohio road map in his back pocket and picks a rural point in the countryside as a destination. Once there, he walks or rides around until he finds a diner and buys a cup of coffee with cream and a slice of pie for lunch. He chooses an alternate route home if there is one.

The party is on a Saturday night and Paul has only work clothes. Though

Mrs. Benton has offered Paul the opportunity to look over a neatly ironed pile of her husband's casual shirts, Paul is uncomfortable with both the idea and the golfing images on the shirts. He declines politely, citing a different size, though he does not know his exact size, as he has always worn either tees or pullover cotton sweaters.

Mrs. Benton tells him of the thrift store in town that is allied with the hospital auxiliary for which she is a volunteer. On a visit there, he selects two pairs of chino slacks and two plain Oxford shirts that look new. He has spent $6.75 on the four articles of clothing. Mrs. Benton makes a big fuss over his purchase and insists that he model them for her, which he does with embarrassment. He is grateful for her care and attentions, but uncomfortable with this sort of display.

Paul arrives at the party a little after six p.m. The light is already beginning to fade, though clocks have not yet been set back. A barbecue is in full swing and the air is rich with the smell of broiling chickens. Two large home-welded steel barbecue pits stand waist-high on legs fashioned from bent rebar.

Several hundred chicken halves compressed between two steel grillwork racks lie smoking above the charcoal embers. Four kegs of beer sit in a cattle watering tank full of ice. Women about bustle banquet tables covered with white tablecloths, laying out plastic knives, forks and paper plates. Other ladies carry in pies and industrial-size kitchen bowls full of coleslaw, potato and pasta salads.

A swing band is tuning up on a small stage made of old pallets and used 4 x 8 sheets of plywood. People in and out of military uniforms are milling about holding drinks and chatting. Paul doesn't know anyone but Freddy and Jerry, whom Freddy has invited as well. Jerry's wife is with him.

"What's your poison?" Freddy asks Paul. "Beer or whiskey?"

"I'll have a beer," smiles Paul.

Freddy goes to the kegs and draws a pint of Iron City into a waxed cup, returning and handing it to Paul.

"The worst, best beer ever made," he says as he hands it to Paul. You'll need two for each Rolling Rock you'd normally drink. Iron City's a little stingy on the alcohol ... 3.2 at best. Does the job, though. You'll just piss a lot. What's your brew at home?"

"Mostly Carling's or Ballantine," Paul answers, recalling the neon signs he has seen glowing in the windows of roadside taverns near home.

Paul stays close to Freddy and Jerry and Jerry's wife. The band is playing swing tunes and a small crowd has gathered around the stage, tapping feet and nodding appreciatively at the music. The dancing will begin in earnest after the barbecue.

Several men linger around the barbecue pits, pointing at the cooking birds, dispensing unsolicited advice about the birds' readiness tobe plated.

"Christ, call a vet! He can still save these birds! They ain't nowhere near cooked!" one card calls out.

Another man walks up and down the racks with a plant sprayer on his back. A tube runs from the tank to the nozzle in his hand. He is spraying the chickens with a reddish barbecue sauce. Jerry sees Paul watching the man spraying the chickens.

"Pretty clever, eh? That's Moody's secret barbecue sauce he's spraying on them birds. He used to be a firefighter and that's an old water sprayer from his fire-fightin' days. Folks invite him for every barbecue: beef, pork, wieners, chicken ... you name it. He brews sauce for 'em all."

The crowd turns to the bandstand as a bugler begins to play the call for assembly. When the bugler formally lowers his instrument, mimicking a salute, a uniformed man bedecked with medals and epaulettes steps to the microphone and welcomes everyone. He, in turn, introduces a uniformed chaplain who leads the silent crowd in a prayer of remembrance. Paul follows suit as many set their beer cups on the ground between their feet and bow their heads in prayer. The benediction is followed by a brief remembrance by the senior military officer and a twenty-one gun salute to the fallen by an honor guard made up of representatives of the all military services. The reverence lasts for several minutes after the ceremony and then the crowd slowly resumes its earlier antic chatter.

Soon a rotund man in a stained apron steps forward and begins banging a tire iron inside a large iron triangle, signaling the crowd to form two lines for dinner. He then joins another man and the two, wielding tongs, set large chicken halves on the thin paper plates, reminding diners to hold their plates from the bottom, "so's not to have to eat red clay chicken."

People come off the last buffet table holding their plates, heaped high with chicken, several salads, and potato chips, with both hands. Some carry their beer cups clenched between their teeth as they walk carefully toward the picnic tables set up in the field nearby.

The band members take a break and fill their own plates and glasses after the last guests move through the line. The heavyset bass player notes appreciatively to the fiddler behind him that there'll be plenty of seconds by his count, as a whole 4 x 4 rack of chicken halves remains above the coals.

When the four rusty steel barrels by the beer kegs are overflowing with paper plates, chicken bones, and napkins, the musicians reassemble on stage, check their tunings with one another, and compare notes about the audience's energy and a suitable song list.

The band strikes up a perennial favorite by Bob Wills and the Texas Playboys, *Spanish Two Step,* and half the assembled rise to their feet. Hands are extended to wives and girlfriends; and, for many, a smiling glance and a nod toward the dance floor are enough to entice a lady to her feet. The portable dance floor is soon full and people spill over onto the recently mowed grass. The band doesn't pause between numbers and goes right into *Sugar Moon.* More people make their way to the dance floor or stake out a place on the grass and, after several numbers, only the elderly and the infirm are still at the picnic tables, nodding appreciatively at the music and the agility of the dancers.

Over the course of a half dozen up-tempo dance numbers, some couples walk back to their tables, breathing heavily and smiling broadly from the exertion. This opens floor space for the show dance couples, known locally for their dance floor theatrics. They begin with a stately and deceptive promenade and then break suddenly into their show-off swings and twirls, delighting the onlookers. Ladies slide on their heels between the legs of their men and are drawn back out and onto their feet. Trusting girls with flouncing western-style skirts are hoisted high overhead by their partners and set gently back down to the evident appreciation of the onlookers. More formal Lindy Hoppers strut their stuff and a few manic jitterbuggers bring those watching from the sidelines to their feet to watch their heel-and-toe gymnastics.

After a half hour of high-energy dancing, the band slows into *The Tennessee Waltz* and *Blue Moon of Kentucky,* and the young make way for older couples, who stroll hand-in-hand to the dance floor. The men greet their ladies with a bow, take their hands and initiate the first step of a stately waltz. Some husbands smile fondly down at their wives; others are flat of affect and make a point of looking away as if dancing were a social formality or they had been coerced into making a spectacle of themselves.

Paul watches all this from his table. Jerry is waltzing with his wife. Freddy is scanning the crowd for singles. A former schoolmate of Freddy's, recently divorced, has promised to meet him but he has not yet seen her in the crowd. Paul listens distractedly to Freddy's discourse on the new self-leveling transits coming into the market that will obviate the need for a plumb bob, when he feels a tap on his right shoulder. He turns around, half expecting to see Mrs. Benton, and finds himself looking into the doe eyes of a tall girl in jeans and a western-style shirt with pearl buttons.

"Wanna dance?" she asks him before he can say hello.

He smiles and wags his head slightly side to side, hoping to dissuade her. She resets her posture with her arms akimbo and cocks her head as if to say, "Why not? Ain't I pretty enough?"

Remembering his manners, he extracts himself one leg at a time from his position on the picnic bench and turns to face her. He doesn't stand tall but smiles at her.

"I'm not much of a dancer," he says looking at her directly for the first time.

She says, "Most boys aren't but they figure it out eventually. You're not from around here, are you? College boy?"

"I used to be, wasn't much good at that, either. I work construction in the next town."

"Where you from?" she asks.

"Northern Vermont," he answers.

"Farm boy?"

"Aye-yup," he jests, smiling shyly at his courage.

"College-educated farm boy, no less," she returns with an equine toss of her head.

"Well, let's see if this country college girl can teach this farm boy to dance," she says, taking his hand and leading him to a corner of the dance floor.

Paul is conscious. Glenda has told the charge nurse that she believes Paul will be more responsive if there are fewer people for him to contend with by his bedside. Doctor Abrams, who oversees Paul's treatment, endorses her suggestion. Paul's mother volunteers to stay behind if Glenda will promise to fill her in on the details of the conversation and to convey her love to Paul. Glenda agrees.

Dr. Abrams pulls the privacy curtain closed with a swish. The loud noise of its hardware traveling around the oval perimeter frame causes Paul to open his eyes. As he blinks away the narcotic residue, Glenda, Dr. Abrams and a nurse come into view in the cramped space next to his bed. A tubular frame over the bed immobilizes his pelvis and left leg. His right arm and head are also immobilized by a similar apparatus that reminds him of the roll bar on Jerry's bulldozer. His visitors are crowded into his field of vision.

Dr. Abrams addresses Paul first, asking him how he's feeling. Paul tries to smile and answers that, generally, he doesn't. Dr. Abrams smiles in turn and asks Paul if he can feel his legs. Paul says he can't. Dr. Abrams asks him what he can move that doesn't cause pain. Paul moves the fingers of his left hand and then the fingers of his right hand in the cast above his head. He forces a limited range of sideways motion with his head before a snap of pain causes him to wince.

Dr. Abrams asks him a series of non-medical questions for which Glenda has little patience. Paul, however, seems amused by them and answers each: his age, where he lives, his father's name — questions designed to measure his lucidity, which to Glenda, who has spoken with him twice now since the accident, is obvious, though Paul can't answer the question about the date of the accident. Paul senses his sister's impatience and reassures her with a smile that Dr. Abrams' questions aren't annoying him.

The nurse is dutifully recording the medical points of the interrogation.

Dr. Abrams begins to describe to Paul the dimensions of his injuries. He starts with a long list of skeletal injuries: broken arm and clavicle, fractured pelvis, broken leg, and as yet unknown injuries to his left foot and ankle. He also has three cracked ribs. Dr. Abrams then goes on to detail Paul's known internal injuries, explaining that they must do farther tests to understand their full extent. He appears outwardly stable. They have removed his ruptured spleen and restored a collapsed lung punctured by a broken rib. They are worried about peritonitis, but he is showing no sign of a fever.

With an uneasy air of disingenuous familiarity, Dr. Abrams summarizes what he has to say in the familiar "good news, bad news" cliché.

"Unlike in most motorcycle accidents, you did not incur a massive head injury. You were conscious when you were brought into emergency. Most people we see who "go over the bars" are never the same, if they do emerge from a coma. They and their families must learn to live with a new and very different person, often someone who is limited intellectually and emotionally. The bad news is that you have serious spinal injuries. We won't know how serious until we run an EMG. We'll need your help."

It's Paul's turn and he asks, "Will I be able to walk?"

"We won't know until we do the tests. There's a broad spectrum of possible outcomes and sequelae," Dr. Abrams continues, looking away from Paul toward the scanning monitor recording Paul's vital signs, "the worst being

paraplegia and the best being a near full recovery. But it may take years and will certainly require lots of patience on your part."

Dr. Abrams and the nurse soon leave the tented space. Glenda holds Paul's hand and is quiet. Paul interrupts their silence and whispers to Glenda that he is not sure he has it in him.

The band is playing *Your True Love,* a rockabilly song made famous by Carl Perkins. Paul wishes he was back at the picnic table but cannot take his eyes of the girl who has led him onto the dance floor. Her long hazel hair swishes at each dance floor turn. She is beautiful in a way unfamiliar to Paul. Her strong features compose a radiant smile and her eyes are in constant movement, yet seem to focus only on him. He is both flattered and embarrassed.

"My name's Jolinda. People call me Jo for short. What's your handle?"

"Paul," he answers. "People call me Paul for short," he jokes.

She beams a broad smile at him and poses again, akimbo.

"I like you already," she says. "Now this is gonna be easy. You just gotta relax and trust me. Here take my hand, put your hand on this shoulder. I'll show you. Soon you'll be leading me around the dance floor. Here we go."

Paul senses the rhythm of the music and soon picks up the movements by watching Jo and other couples nearby. At first he is embarrassed by the jerky movements he is making, but when he looks up at Jo and sees her smiling approvingly at him, his discomfort goes away and he listens to the rockabilly music and dances.

"You're a natural," Jo shouts over the music at him and he smiles.

After several dances, the two retreat from the dance floor and walk back to his table, where he introduces Jo to Jerry and his wife. Freddy has apparently found his divorcée and disappeared. Jo offers to get a new round of beers. As she leaves, Jerry winks appreciatively at Paul, with an eye on the conscious wag of Jo's departing tail and asks, "Who's your new honey? She's a cutie pie." Jo soon returns, nestling two cups in her arms and two in her hands.

The band takes a break after the next set, a relaxed alternation of waltzes and two-steps. Jerry yawns hard and offers his good night. He nods politely to Jo and leaves with his wife in tow.

Jo slides closer to Paul on the bench and asks, "So who are you? You married?"

Paul smiles at the question. He is flattered at the assumption and answers with a smile and a two-syllable, "no-oo."

"Got a girlfriend?" Jo persists.

"Just Mrs. Benton," Paul says with mock seriousness.

"You havin' it on with a married woman!?" Jo says, rearing back.

"No," he laughs out loud. Mrs. Benton is the only woman in my life right now. She's my landlady. She's 72 and owns the boarding house where I stay. She is a widow, though, so there's possibilities."

Jo laughs out loud and puts her arm around Paul's shoulder. "I like you," she offers close up.

"Me, too," Paul answers. "I mean I like you, too."

The band picks up again, a tune by the Blue Sky Boys called *Turn Your Radio On*. When the song is through, the lead singer steps to the mike and announces, "Now we'd like to do a few of our gospel favorites for the few saints in the crowd. We've entertained you sinners long enough and now it's time to come to Jesus and hear the word of the Lord." The band breaks into an old-time gospel number called *The Royal Telephone*:

Central's never busy,
always on the line;
You may hear from heaven
almost any time;

'Tis a royal service,
free for one and all;
When you get in trouble,
give this royal line a call.

"Love this crap," says Jo, staring out over her beer cup.
After the last bent notes of the pedal steel fade, the band's lead vocalist again steps to the mike and says, "And now I'd like to ask an old friend and a great singer to join us for an up-tempo rendition of *Angel Band*. Jo come on up on stage and sing us a song or two."

"Oh, shit! I shoulda known this'd happen. Be right back."

Stunned, Paul sets his beer down on the warped picnic table and turns to watch Jo extract herself from the bench and walk to the stage while the audience applauds.

The fiddle and rhythm guitar introduce the theme. The dobro, bass and pedal steel join in and the band plays an instrumental chorus before Jo steps forward, wraps her right hand around the mike and begins:

My latest sun is sinking fast. My race is nearly run.
My strongest trials now are past. My triumph has begun.

Oh, come, angel band, come and around me stand
Bear me away on your snowy wings to my immortal home.

I've almost gained my heavenly home. My spirit loudly sings.
The holy ones, behold, they come. I hear the noise of wings.

O, come, angel band.....

Paul watches his new friend, rapt by the surprisingly deep alto and her ease in front of the audience of strangers. The band members grin ear-to-ear and the audience bursts into loud applause when Jo steps back from the mike and nods gratefully to the cheering crowd.

A shout rings out from the audience, "*Canaan's Land.*" Jo looks at the fiddler who nods back to her and she leads off a cappella:

To Canaan's land I'm on my way
  Where the soul (of man) never dies
My darkest night will turn to day
  Where the soul (of man) never dies

  No sad farewells
  (And, friend, there'll be no sad farewells)
  No tear-dimmed eyes
  (There'll be no tear-dimmed eyes)
  Where all is peace
  (Where all is peace and joy and love)
  And the soul (of man) never dies

A love light burns across the foam
And shines to light the shores of home

A rose is blooming there for me
And I will spend eternity
Where the soul of man never dies.

In the call and response chorus, Jo is joined by the stand-up bass player, who leans into another mike and harmonizes each echoed line in a rich baritone.

Jo again nods to the audience in gratitude as they applaud loudly while she makes her way back across the dance floor and lawn to Paul who is smiling broadly. Several "Ye-has" and lusty wolf whistles punctuate the sustained applause. Paul realizes that the woman for whom this adulation is intended is walking across the open dance floor toward him.

"Y'a like that? I know plenty more. I love those old gospel harmonies. I like other songs, too, but gospel's the most fun to sing. Let's have another beer and go back to my place. I'll show you were I live. It's not far. It's getting late and we both have to work tomorrow."

Paul wakes up in the middle of the night, though time has lost much of its meaning. His position on the hospital bed now enables him to see out of the corner of his eye the green neon-framed Lumichron clock on the far wall.

Until now, only the arrangement of vapid foods on a scratched Melamine plate waiting to be spooned into him by a distracted orderly has offered any hint of diurnal time. The feeding tube was removed on the fifth day, as the drugs being given him to maintain a coma state were withdrawn.

Glenda is curled up in a patient chair on the side that he can see near the foot of the bed. She is sleeping, but does not look comfortable. Her body forms a comma and her head rests on her arm above the wooden armrest. The chair has an adjustable back which is lowered as far back as it will go. The look on Glenda's face betrays her discomfort in the unforgiving chair.

Paul watches her, recalling different times in their childhood that return to him as cinematic vignettes. There is no discernible dialogue, but the articulate visual details and the feelings they summon recall for Paul the narrative of their time together in that place. He and Glenda picking their way down the steep talus path off Mount Hor with Uncle Theron leading the way and eyeing the lowering sky; Glenda telling Paul with tears in her eyes that she has been accepted at McGill and Paul's confusion as to whether they are tears of relief, joy or sadness at the knowledge that their lives will now diverge; swimming side-by-side in Lake Willoughby and in Long Pond with only the splashing sound of their synchronous strokes plowing the wind-rippled water; their daily walks to meet the school bus at the end of the road or their walks home, often in the dark of a late winter afternoon.

Paul makes no sound. The contentment he feels just looking at Glenda surprises him. When they were young, it was hard for him to be without her company and, when he awoke, he would immediately try to wake her as well. When she was thirteen and her changing body needed more sleep to transform her into a woman, he half-heartedly agreed to let her sleep in on Sunday, tiptoeing downstairs and busying himself with his mother until Glenda came down the steep, narrow attic stairway ready for the day.

Paul wakes up the next morning early. Jo is beside him in the disheveled bed and the room is filled with the unfamiliar scent of their intimacy. Paul is aware that he drank more than he ever has, and he suddenly fears that which he might not remember. But as he lies there quietly, watching Jo sleep, the evening returns to him.

He has always assumed that males initiate sex. His few male friends at school boasted of their conquests, leading him to believe that his role would be to overcome the natural defenses of any girl with whom he wanted to have sex. They had also, along with his parents, instilled in him a fear of an out-of-wedlock pregnancy, both for the boy and for the unwed mother-to-be.

It had not happened that way, though. Paul followed Jo back to her apartment in a town twelve miles away. The two sat up until two in the morning talking to one another, mostly about where they grew up, their families and what the intervening years had brought since they left home.

Jo had grown up in a religious family. She could not remember a time when her family did not attend church together on Sunday or on religious holidays. She had been "sanctified" at an early age in her white dress, "choosing the Lord" at the age of five.

As she discovered her own maturing body, her enthusiasm for the moral rigors of the Ohio Baptist Convention waned in favor of the social and physical pleasures she began to read about in magazines, imagine and later experience. She maintained, however, a demure facade for her parents while setting out alone to explore her own life at fourteen. The sole passion she retained from her fervent religious upbringing was for the "radio songs" the family listened to on their Emerson console radio after supper on Sunday. She began singing along as a young girl and, by ten, had soon committed to memory the verses of several dozen of the white gospel songs

Much against the will of her parents who had planned for her to attend Wheaton College in Illinois, Jolinda applied secretly to Antioch in Ohio and was accepted. She accepted and applied for financial assistance. Only when the financial aid forms were sent to her father did her parents learn of her decision and throw her out. Seventeen, she took refuge with a sympathetic aunt who lived in a Boston marriage in Jamestown, New York, with a local librarian.

The freestyle life at college appealed to Jolinda. She made no effort to reconnect with her family. In the spring semester, her mother lost control of the family car returning from a tent gathering in Columbus and died in the ambulance. Jolinda returned home and was greeted warmly, if tearfully, by her father, whom she had always suspected of having less religious fervor than her mother.

The "calling hours" and the funeral service again imposed on the young woman the rectitude of her childhood. She saw in family and former friends the recriminatory looks she had often suffered as a young girl.

Now, unable to muster a grief-stricken mien or tears, Jolinda kept her head bowed throughout the service. But when the organist played the opening notes of *Shall We Gather at the River*, Jolinda, to the embarrassment of the few attending relatives on her mother's side and many in the congregation, lifted her head and sang along with the confused choir above and behind her in the choir loft in full-throated bluegrass harmony.

The stern minister seemed to his flock to be concealing a smile and her father looked at her with evident pride.

Jolinda did not recount to Paul much after the death of her mother, except to say that she had traveled for several months with an old-timey band as a harmony singer and had had a "flirtation" with the lead singer and guitarist.

Shortly thereafter, Jo rose from the couch where they had been sitting and led Paul to her bedroom. She disappeared into the bathroom, returned to the bedroom without clothes, removed Paul's clothes with abandon and settled onto Paul as if he were a rodeo pony.

At a loss, Paul tried in vain to remember what he had heard from his more experienced friends at home about sexual conquest.

"Just relax," Jo said, sensing his confusion.

He said nothing, relieved by the futility of his position beneath her and surprised at the speed with which Jo achieved her own pleasure on top of him. Paul had never seen a woman in orgasm and when her light trembling ended and she collapsed forward onto his chest, she assured him that he would enjoy the same pleasure. She dropped down next to him and laid her head on his chest with her breasts nestled in his arms and took him on an outsider's tour of his own familiar anatomy, demonstrating for him the difference in sexual stimulation between the top of his penis and the underneath.

"It is the top that pleasures us girls, while it's the bottom part that works you broncos into a froth," she told him in a school-marmish tone. She mounted him again and within several minutes he had experienced the same pleasure Jo had, the rolling motion of her hips exciting that part of him that she had told him was most pleasurable.

Paul looks at Jolinda. She is sleeping deeply. Her respiration produces light susurrus through her slightly parted lips. Her dark hair cascades over the pillow on which a smudge of lipstick has stained the pillowcase. Her facial features twitch and her demeanor changes as if she is in a fugal state. He is enthralled by the beautiful woman lying next to him.

A large Big Ben alarm clock, showing 6:17 a.m., ticks loudly on her bedside table. A brilliant rising sun radiates light into the drawn shade. Paul wonders if Jolinda sets her clock ahead in order to be on time. He tries to calculate the miles to the jobsite and whether he would be back-tracking the sum of the two distances or whether Jolinda's apartment might in fact be on the way. He suddenly remembers Mrs. Benton and worries what she will infer from his absence at breakfast. He has not called, though she knew he was going to the party.

Paul arises carefully to put on coffee, take a shower and then wake up Jolinda, as he doesn't know what time she has to be at work. As his right foot alights, Jolinda's groggy voice asks, "Where ya going, partner?"

"Put on the coffee?" Paul asks.

"Sounds good," Jolinda says, sitting up naked in bed. "I have to be at work at eight and I can't go like this. Smells like a fish cannery in here. Let's take a shower, save water. Put the coffee on and hustle back. I'll turn on the hot water, takes a few minutes in this apartment complex, tank heater's in the basement...bathrobe on the hook on the door.... picture window in the kitchen. Don't want this place looking to the neighbors like a house of ill repute. I'm upstanding," she continues, standing up and walking naked into the bathroom.

Paul hears water running as he looks for a coffee pot in the kitchen.

Jolinda is wringing her hair in the generous flow of warm water. He is surprised at the surfeit of black pubic hair hiding her nudity and the upright generosity of her breasts with their dark aureoles. He remembers with some embarrassment her invitation to kiss them and the extraordinary pleasure she seemed to take from his labial attentions. She sees Paul looking at her appreciatively and makes room in the cramped shower stall for him. Paul steps in and redraws the cotton curtain. Jolinda turns to face him. She mistakes the confluence of his sadness and gratitude as modesty and draws him to her under the cascade of warmth. She reassures him that their intimacy is okay and cannot see the tears in his eyes. Paul is overwhelmed by the realization that this woman in the shower is drawn to him and he allows himself to be held closely.

Paul is listening to a litany of medical jargon. He imagines himself in the back of a large lecture hall with a few students randomly seated around the steep descent to a stage and dais far below him where a white-coated man is speaking. Glenda is sitting several tiers below him and off to his left. She is paying attention to the man speaking and taking notes. Paul wants to get her attention, but cannot. He closes his eye.

"Are you tired, Paul, or are you experiencing pain?" a disturbingly close voice asks. Paul opens his eye and is facing an unfamiliar doctor with a retinue of other doctors in green scrubs and a nurse clutching his chart to her substantial bosom. Paul blinks to clear his vision and looks quizzically at the doctor, who is awaiting a response to his question.

"Where's my sister?" Paul asks in answer to the doctor's question.

"I'm sorry. I don't know your sister," the doctor answers, with an interrogatory glance at the nurse, who answers for him.

"She had to go back to college. Your mother and father will be here later this afternoon."

Paul appears fatigued by this news and again closes his eye.

"Let me see his chart," the doctor says to the nurse.

"Who prescribed Haldol?" he asks.

"Dr. Loomis was on call last night," the nurse responds.

"Have there been any problems with this patient indicating a need for Haldol?" the doctor continues, clearly annoyed.

"Not to my knowledge, Doctor," the nurse answers.

"Suspend it immediately. No further psychotropics ordered without my written permission. He's immobilized and can't injure himself. If he becomes agitated, call me. Enter that notation on the chart."

"Yes, Doctor Sametz," the nurse answers without looking up from the chart on which she is making the notation.

Paul hears their departing footsteps. He is not sure what he has heard or from whom. Nor can he decipher what the doctor was saying to him or to those on rounds with him. He remembers only hearing the nurse say that Glenda has returned to McGill.

He wanted to tell her that he has begun having sudden phobic reactions to being immobilized, that he has begun to feel neural pain from his immobile limbs, and that the anti-itch medicine is no longer effective, but the Haldol has limited the expression of his sequestered thoughts and fears to grunting noises and his attempts at thought are raveling.

"So, was the party fun?" Mrs. Benton asks with a sly look at her lodger.

"Very fun," Paul answers. "Good music and food and lots of dancing."

"There's always good music and dancing at those VFW wingdings. Mr. Benton and I would go every year. We could go free because he was a member. We'd have such fun dancing. We weren't much on the drinking, but I'd have a glass or sometimes two of sherry with my dinner, and Mr. Benton would have a beer," she says with a twinkle.

"Hope you found some dance partners," she adds.

"Oh, I did," he answers.

"There's always plenty of young gals there looking for a handsome fella like you," Mrs. Benton adds merrily.

Paul helps Mrs. Benton clear the table and makes his way up the stairs, grateful that she did not ask him where he spent the previous night.

Jolinda comes to Paul throughout the day in imagined stills. These, however, are life stills, not the gaudy centerfold images that Danny kept by his bed at Bowling Green.

He pauses occasionally and smiles, still surprised and grateful that she chose him to be with. The enduring afterglow and recall of his first love-making slows his hand today as a laborer, as he unloads bales of asphalt roofing shingles from a flatbed truck, cutting away the steel banding with a tinsnip, and handing smaller bunches up to another laborer who lays them out in piles around the roof sheathing. The roofers will then apply them from the eaves up to the ridgeline. He can think only of seeing Jolinda again. The folded piece of paper in his wallet bears her phone number, his only link to her.

At breakfast he learned that she works in a record store in Defiance and three evenings a week for her father, a local attorney, where she is clerking to become a lawyer. It's seventeen miles to where she lives and Paul worries about his motorcycle. Recently, the motor has been suddenly losing power and sputtering erratically. Then it catches again and returns to full RPMs until the next time. He wants to believe it's bad gas or the carburetor needs cleaning but he knows the valves are going, though that would not explain its random power losses.

At day's end, he phones Mrs. Benton to say only that he will be staying with a friend and she should not make dinner for him. He worries she will miss his company.

He's a few miles from Jolinda's and a heavy mist hangs in the air. Though it is not raining, the mist soaks through his denim jacket and T-shirt. His bike is behaving erratically. As he leaves the stop sign at a crossroads, the bike stalls as he clicks the gear lever down into first and releases the clutch. He soon realizes that no amount of kicking or tinkering is going to restart the bike. He moves it to the side of the road and begins hitchhiking into Defiance. Several cars pass him and then a rusty Ford Country Squire wagon pulls up and the driver signals him to get in with a wave of his hand.

"You headed for Defiance or beyond?" the driver asks.

"Defiance is fine," Paul answers. "Thanks for the lift. I think my bike may have finally died."

"What kind? Looked English to me. Them English bikes take a lot of tinkering. If you're not the tinkering type, they're a pain in the ass. I got me a Honda ... runs like a top, never had any trouble with her. People love them English bikes, never understood why. It's like my brother-in-law, has a '53 MG TD. Why? I ask you. Yah, it looks fun with its two little leather seats and its luggage rack on the back, but under the hood's a nightmare. Ought to come with a mechanic in the trunk if you ask me but you didn't, did you? You from Defiance?"

"Vermont," Paul answers, "just working construction out here for the summer."

"My wife's cousin's folks hale from Bennington. You might know 'em."

"I'm from the northern part, up near Canada. Bennington's in the southwestern corner, long way away from there," Paul explains.

"I thought Vermont was small and everyone knew everyone else," the driver insists, looking at Paul.

"Some towns are that way, but the state's pretty spread out," Paul responds, content to let the voluble driver direct the conversation and noticing that the mist has turned into a downpour.

"Like Appalachia, I bet," the driver opines, this time without looking at Paul.

"Maybe. Never been there," Paul answers.

"I can just get off up there by the diner," Paul says, recognizing the neighborhood.

"Thanks a lot for the lift. It would've been a mighty wet hike into town. Thanks again."

"You ever need any insurance, any kind at all, you call Bud Emmons. Here's my card. Keep it in your wallet, and, take my advice, get yourself a Jap bike, run like a top. Y'all take care, now, and don't do anyone I wouldn't do," he says with a wink that distorts the whole right side of his face. Paul gets out of the car with a wave back to the driver who waves at him as he pulls away.

Paul waits in the rain until the taillights of the station wagon are out of sight. He then crosses the street and enters the diner. In the warmth of the diner, he removes his wet jacket, sets it down on the stool next to him, and waits for the busy waitress's attention.

"What'll it be, son?" the waitress asks, walking by him with two plates of food. "Menu's right next to you there by the jukebox console. Blue Plate Special today is fried clams and fries. Be right back."

On her return, Paul orders two cheeseburgers to go with a side each of coleslaw and fries.

"Up in three minutes. Coffee while you wait?" she answers.

"Sure, thanks," answers Paul, "with a splash of cream."

"Creamer's by the jukebox. Help yourself."

The waitress sets a heavy ironstone mug of coffee in front of him and goes about her business.

Holding his wet jacket over his head with one hand and clutching the warm grease-stained bag in his other, Paul walks to Jolinda's. By arrangement, this is her night home and he hopes she'll be there as promised so he won't have to wait in the hall.

Inside what was once a large Victorian, Paul climbs the stairs to her apartment, tries the door, and walks in, expecting to find Jolinda. The apartment is empty although the door is unlocked. He sets the surprise supper in the kitchen, goes into the bathroom and takes a hot shower. He leaves his wet shirt to dry on a towel rack and settles in the living room, feeling uncomfortable, alone in someone else's apartment. He picks up a local weekly and looks through the classifieds, knowing that he will have to spring for either an old car or another beater bike. He sees an array of late model Japanese bikes, a Triumph Bonneville, Norton Atlas, an Ariel Square Four, and a column's length of Harleys.

The next thing Paul senses is a prolonged kiss on the mouth. He opens his eyes suddenly to see Jolinda smiling at him.

"Not a bad alarm clock, am I? What's for supper? I could eat you raw," she says, throwing her rough-out leather jacket on the couch.

"I got some stuff at the diner, nothing fancy. I was hungry, too, glad you're hungry. Just need to put the burgers in the toaster oven," he says, rubbing his eyes.

"What are you gonna have? I see you got me a couple of cheeseburgers. The slaw must be for you. I don't eat vegetables unless they're cooked or covered with gravy. You should have asked Ginny at the diner for a pint of gravy with the fries. It's free. My favorite ... gravy on fries. Just kidding about the cheeseburgers. Good of you to get this stuff," she said, returning to the living room with two green, long-necked bottles of Rolling Rock.

"Hard day at the office?"

"Bike died on the way here, had to hitch. Got a ride with an insurance salesman who talked all the way here."

"Bud Emmons," Jolinda laughs. "An old friend of my dad's, he can talk your ear off. Did he sell you any insurance? I guess it's a bit late now that your bike's dead. Where'd you bury it?"

"I've never had any insurance. It's about six miles outside of town, 'longside the road," Paul says. "I'll have to pick it up 'cause they'll track the registration to me."

"I know a guy who builds bikes for local kids. He may have something for you. I'll call him from work tomorrow and ask him what he's got. He may even take your bike, if it's there in the morning, as a parts bike in trade. What're you gonna do when winter comes?" she says, looking askance at him as if he has never considered this.

"Get a snow tire, I guess." he answers.

Jolinda giggles at his joke and suggests they go to bed. It is still light.

In bed, Paul confesses his lack of sexual experience to Jolinda, but does not admit that their previous night together was his first experience with a woman. Jolinda feigns surprise, and then shows Paul the source of her pleasure, encouraging his aggression, though he is tentative and afraid of making a mistake.

In the hospital, Paul will often remember this evening, not for the sexual encounter, but for the deep sense of well-being he feels at being held and for the whispered conversation lasting deep into the night.

It has not occurred to Paul to ask to see himself in a mirror. Bandages have been removed from his face, but there is still one over his left eye and his chin is badly bruised though not broken. The road rash on his left cheek has begun to heal into black-blood furrows that will leave him with livid scars.

Thoughts, memories and dreams are coming more clearly now that he is no longer given Haldol, but the claustrophobia of immobility now overwhelms him in the middle of the night.

He awakes from a dream in which he and Jolinda are back in the small roadside bar where she often sings with a pickup group of string players she knows. He dreams sometimes of lying next to Jolinda late at night and of her singing quietly to him her favorite coal mining ballads from Virginia,

West Virginia and Kentucky. The melodies, if not the words of Payday at Coal Creek, Dark as a Dungeon and Blue Diamond Mines are all still familiar to him.

But the unbidden fear strikes more often now and is made worse by the sensory deprivation in the intensive care unit.

Paul and Glenda are in second and third grades. It is an overcast morning and they have finished their Saturday chores. The smell of bleach is still on Glenda's hands from hanging out the week's laundry in the back yard. Paul's hands still smell of the chicken manure and mulch hay he has just mucked out of the chicken coop. The two are standing far below a dirt road on the mossy bank of Blodgett Brook. The lines from their fish poles slice the slow-running current. They are trying to entice the small brook trout out from under the moss overhang on which they are standing with worms they have just gathered from turning over a dead tree trunk moldering nearby.

Paul is impatient and suggests to his older sister that they try the banks on the other side of the road. Glenda urges her impatient brother to wait. After another fifteen minutes without even a nibble, Glenda acquiesces and agrees to try the other side where the stream undercuts the bank even more.

Looking up at the road high above them, Paul suggests they wriggle through the culvert that carries the brook underneath the road bed high above. Glenda looks skeptical and says she doesn't want to get wet. Paul suggests a race and Glenda agrees.

In his dream however, he does not beat Glenda to the other side as he did when they were little. In his dream he enters the culvert on his hands and knees, but soon must lie down in the trickle of water and slither forward toward the light on the other side. The diameter of the culvert seems, though, to be getting narrower as he progresses and he must choose whether to keep his hands in front of him or by his side and push himself through the with his feet. He chooses the latter and pushes with his wet sneakers. He soon finds himself stuck in the culvert and can no longer go forward or backward with just his legs, as the sandy gravel offers his wet sneakers no purchase.

He hears Glenda calling to him from far down the other end, but in his dream he cannot call back. The words do not seem to emerge from his mouth although he hears them in his mind. The oncoming trickle of water is rising slowly as he has blocked its flow to the other side. He tries in vain to move his arms, but they are pinned by the culvert to the side of his body. He panics. He can neither yell out to Glenda nor dislodge himself from the constriction of the culvert.

He wakes up in a cold sweat, still trying to escape, but this time it is not the culvert immobilizing him but the traction and partial body cast.

Paul's motor impulses call up a panicked exertion to break free. Cerebral neurotransmitters emit muscle commands but there is no reaction in his dependent limbs, the movements of which seem only a memory. The panic accelerates to terror. Awake now, Paul closes his eyes and tries to breathe deeply as he has been told to do, but he is no longer capable of the equanimity he has so often experienced with Jolinda or, earlier, with Glenda at his side. Like an empty silo, his mind fills up with questions he has been unable to articulate. He tries to remember them all.

Dr. Abrams rounds once a day, and the nurse who checks on him is otherwise occupied and dismissive, telling him to save his questions for Dr. Abrams, who is managing his case. But he is not always able to remember them or conscious when the doctor appears at his bedside.

Paul thinks only of leaving the hospital but worries that he has lost the mobility to do so and doesn't yet know why.

The following day after work, Jolinda drives Paul to Hilger's Chop Shop just outside Defiance. There is no indication from the road that this is a business. The open, single-car garage attached to a blue raised ranch disgorges into the driveway and front lawn a clutter of engine blocks, empty motorcycle frames, and half-assembled motorcycles. Inside, Paul can see a motorcycle lift, and two four-foot, roll-around tool chests. The back wall is a makeshift wooden shelf sagging under the weight of knucklehead, panhead and shovelhead Harley engine blocks in various states of restoration.

Hilger is a tall man with an equatorial beer belly, a full nicotine-tinged beard, bald pate, and a silver ponytail. A restored 1946 *Indian Chief* in resplendent red with new decals and deeply valanced fenders sits on the front lawn leaning into its kickstand. A 2 x 10 slab of pine plank keeps the kickstand from sinking into the lawn, still spongy from recent rains. Next to it, a black Triumph Thunderbird sits upright on its drop-down stand. On the concrete walkway leading to the front door of the house, a Harley Duo-Glide is parked, its powder blue finish almost matching the faded paint on the house. These appear to be the only fully fledged bikes Hilger is offering for sale.

Jolinda greets Hilger like the old friend he is. "Hilger plays mandolin with me sometimes. I learned more songs from Hilger than from the church choir I sang in."

Jolinda gives Hilger a long embrace and a buss on his furry cheek.

"Meet my new friend, Paul. He's from Ver-mont, workin' construction over near Napoleon off the Township Road, converting cornfields to row houses, but we don't hold that against him."

Paul nods to Hilger and smiles.

"Jo says your bike died. What was it?" Hilger asks.

"A Beesa one-lunger. The valves are shot, losing power ever since I bought it. It's a few miles outside of town," Paul answers.

"Hopefully. Let's go see. Get in my truck," Hilger says.

"I'll stay here, if you don't mind," says Jo, "Can't say I want to ride with that floor shift between my legs and you galoots talking cycles over my head. Any coffee inside, Hilger?"

"Help yourself. Just don't disturb the dishes in the sink. I'm aging 'em for supper," Hilger says with a broad smile, evident only in his eyes. There's a new *Biker* mag in there. I don't wanna see any missing from my pile when I get back. I counted 'em," Hilger says, laughing out loud.

To Paul's surprise and anger, the bike is indeed gone. On the way back, Hilger tells Paul that the bike will end up at his place anyway.

"Some farm kid'll come in and try and sell me parts from it. I'll see that you get credit for it. Ain't worth much, but it's still yours. What you looking to buy? I've got some more finished bikes you ain't see'd yet in the lean-to behind the garage," Hilger continues.

"Just some reliable transportation. I'm gonna have to make it back to Vermont before winter. I need more power, too. I can't get outta my own way with that Beesa. I need something with some torque to steer clear of highway trouble," Paul adds.

"You got 600 bucks, I got just the bike for you, finished it a month ago. It's got a ton of torque, takes the road well. It's a hard tail, but I can put a good seat on it for the same price. I'll show it to you when we get back. It's a '49 panhead chopper, best engine Harley ever built ... reliable, starts easy and runs like a rabbit, not like the knuckles and shovels."

"Sounds great. I've got the money, but that doesn't leave me much. I been saving a good deal from my job, but I owe my landlady a month's rent," Paul explains.

"Christ, move in with Jo, she likes ya. She told me. That bitch she had before went out west. Won't be missing her," Hilger hissed.

Paul leaves the confusing comment hanging between them in the truck.

As they drive up, Jolinda is sitting on the Duo-Glide looking quizzically at the Biker Babe centerfold in *Easyriders* magazine, almost as if she is trying to match the woman's pose.

Hilger strides over to her.

"If you ask me, she looks like she belongs on a Honda 50 ... no jugs," Jolinda says to Hilger.

"I didn't ask you. And besides, some people like 'em that way," Hilger answers with a smile.

"Not me," says Jolinda, stuffing the magazine into a fringed saddlebag on the Harley's rear wheel.

"Follow me," says Hilger to Paul, and the two walk around behind the garage.

"That one there," indicates Hilger pointing at a freshly painted black chopper.

"She's a beaut, built from the frame up, hard tail frame, Keihin carb, S&S oil pump, and ape hangers. I've probably put a few hundred miles on it. She rides well, takes corners at speed, except when it's wet. She's not inspectable so I'm just gonna give you a sticker. You can fill it out and put it on yourself. Just don't tell anyone where you got it. Take her for a ride," Hilger says, mounting the bike and turning the key that's already in the ignition.

He pumps the starter lever carefully with his right boot until he feels the full compression, opens the choke and jumps on the bike, which starts with a roar. Hilger backs the choke off half way and lets go of the throttle. The bike drops back to a throaty idle. Paul is surprised at the noise coming from the upswept straight pipes. Jo comes around the corner.

"Now, there's the bike for you. Let's go for a ride, Paul," Jolinda shouts over the throbbing idle of the engine.

Hilger dismounts, opens up the choke and boosts the throttle a bit. He pushes the bike around front to the driveway and leaves it idling for Paul and Jolinda.

"Go on, you two; have fun. Not all day, though. I wanna see you back here in an hour. Bring cash. And, by the way, it's one down and four up. Careful, you're not used to an extended front fork. Take your turns slowly 'til you get used to it." Hilger yells over his shoulder, heading back into the garage.

Paul mounts the bike. Jo climbs on back behind him and wraps her arms around his waist. She realizes the passenger pegs are still up and leans over to push them down on either side. Paul looks back to see if she's ready and stares into her cleavage.

"I'm ready," she says. "Take it easy. I've never been on anything this size."

"Me, neither," admits Paul.

124

Paul kicks up the kickstand with his toe, balances the bike with both feet, and then inclines it slightly to his right side. He withdraws the clutch with his left hand, surprised at the strength it requires to fully engage. He pops the left gear lever down, hears the clunk of the gears engaging, and slowly releases the clutch. The bike sails out of the yard with a roar. Jolinda lets out a yell as they head off down the road.

Paul has never experienced torque. A slight rotation of his right hand and the bike surges forward, eating up the road. He has never ridden such a responsive motorcycle. The lack of any suspension heightens his sense of contact with the asphalt flying beneath him. Jolinda grips him tightly as they speed off into the Ohio countryside, the 84-cubic-inch V-twin roaring between his legs.

Jolinda yells into his left ear to hightail it out of town as the local sheriff has a thing about loud motorcycles and people who ride them. Paul downshifts into a turn out of town and into farm country. The badly cracked and heaved pavement looks as if it has been rearranged by a recent earthquake, and the heaves and potholes telescope the front fork extension erratically. As Paul hits newer sections of pavement, he tries out higher gears and soon becomes used to the shifting pattern and wider turning radius of the chopper.

The road passes several fields separated by windrows and then enters a wooded area. Paul feels the temperature drop several degrees and the scent of open farm land shifts on his next breath to a marshy woodland smell. Jolinda tightens her grip on him and rests her chin on his right shoulder. Below the engine noise he can hear her humming loudly to herself, but cannot make out the song.

After half an hour, they return to Hilger, who doesn't look up as Paul banks the bike into the cluttered drive. Jolinda dismounts, followed by Paul, who closes the ignition and fuel line, and kicks down the stand.

"What a ride!" says Jolinda.

"I'll bring ya the money tomorrow," says Paul. "It's a great bike. I wasn't thinking of anything this big, but it rides great and I love the torque. What's it gonna need to be legal?"

"Don't even ask," says Hilger, not looking up from the tool he is burnishing with a spray of sparks on a fine-grit grinding wheel. "That bike's never gonna be legal, but no cop's gonna know why. They ain't that smart. You just have to have a sticker on there. Fill it out by hand. That's all they look for."

"What happens when it runs out?" asks Paul.

"Any good chop shop'll give you a new one. Some ask a fiver for 'em, but no one'll deny ya."

"If Jolinda can spare me another ride, I'll bring you the cash tomorrow."

"No need to use her. You can take the bike and bring me the cash tomorrow or the next day. I ain't goin' anywhere and if Jolinda likes you, you ain't, either."

Jolinda smiles.

Paul starts up the bike on the first kick and follows Jolinda in her truck out of the yard. Paul is still surprised at Hilger's trust in him to return with the money, but he knows that Jolinda's friendship with Hilger has inspired it. Back at Jolinda's the two share the last beer in the fridge.

Paul tells Jolinda that he has to go to Mrs. Benton's and explain his new circumstances. Jolinda invites Paul to stay with her for a time and save the rent he is paying until he restores some of his savings. He notes that it is not an open-ended invitation, but is surprised and grateful, as he has never been invited by a woman to move in with her.

"Would you like to meet Mrs. Benton?" Paul asks.

Jolinda says, "Sure, but let's take my truck so she doesn't think you've joined Hell's Angels. Besides, riding bitch on that hardtail of yours on these roads is like going to a drunken chiropractor—makes that spring-shot bench-seat in my pickup truck feel like a feather bed."

Paul uses Jolinda's phone to call Mrs. Benton to let her know that he is coming by to visit and to introduce his new friend, but that he will not be staying. He leaves the rest of his news to tell her in person.

Mrs. Benton welcomes Jolinda warmly and hints to her at the maternal role she has been playing to "her well-brought-up visitor from Vermont."

"I'll be sad to lose Paul," she says to Jolinda as if Paul were not in the room, "but happy to know I am losing him to a pretty girl like you," she adds with a sincere smile.

"He's not like my usual lot of guests. It's been a joy having him here and I'm sorry to be losing his company and his good manners. Not for the money, of course, 'cause I can always rent the room, but just 'cause he's such a fine young man," she says, finally turning to acknowledge his presence in the room.

Paul is embarrassed. Jolinda smiles broadly and refrains from making the louche comment that occurs to her.

Paul settles up with Mrs. Benton in cash and promises to take her up on her open-ended invitation to the two to come by for a Sunday dinner whenever they can.

On their return to Jolinda's, Paul worries that the bike he has not yet paid for might be stolen and asks Jolinda if there is a place he can hide it until he buys a length of log chain and a trucker's padlock. Jolinda says the sagging one-car garage appended to the side of the apartment house goes with the downstairs apartment, but the old lady renting the downstairs has no car and will not mind if they hide the bike there.

"She'll never know if you just keep the door shut. She never goes in there."

"Shouldn't we ask her?" asks Paul.

"No," says Jolinda. "She'll just try and think of reasons not to let you. Besides, she's deaf as a post. It'll take all night to ask the question."

Paul is again surprised by the speed with which Jolinda satisfies herself astride him, though she always assures that he, too, is pleasured in the same way. Paul has always imagined lovemaking as a slow acceleration of physical intimacy and wonders, but does not ask, if this is how, in fact, most people make love. He had also imagined that sexual love must be consummated in both partners simultaneously rather than at different times and wonders now if that is indeed required for the act of creation to occur as a friend had once told him. He is beginning to understand how little he has known about physical love and its various pleasures and wonders if Glenda is having a similar experience in Canada in spite of her protestations that she would save herself for a husband.

Paul remembers how much he liked to get in bed at night and draw the cool, rough sheets over his head and lie under them until his young boy's body finally infused the sheets and the depression in his lumpy mattress with his own warmth. On rare occasions and only when invited, he and Glenda would warm one another. Remembering those times now brings tears to his eyes because, although he is never cold now, the plaster and steel mechanics of pendant immobility preclude any exchange of physical warmth. He remembers, too, the warmth generated by his and Jolinda's lovemaking and how, afterwards, they would often throw off the warm sheets to let their bodies cool together in the warm summer breeze coming in the window in Jolinda's bedroom. Paul wonders if he will ever be held again.

It's Saturday morning. Jolinda is drenched in sweat and wakes into stifling heat. As she peels a clingy top sheet from her skin and rises to make coffee, she looks back at Paul in his underpants, still asleep and lying flat on his stomach. Jolinda admires the musculature in his limbs and back and how that musculature sculpts his buttocks. She realizes how much she likes being with Paul. Unlike several earlier boyfriends, Paul understands that there are things he hasn't experienced and he doesn't seem ashamed. He is eager to learn the ways of the world and Jolinda relishes being his teacher in these things.

The clang of cups and the rattle of Jolinda's filling and assembling her old enamel percolator wake Paul up.

"I had no idea it got this hot here," he observes, trudging into the bathroom. "Anyplace around here to swim?"

"What'd you have in mind? A creek, a lake?"

"Any swimming holes in brooks?"

"Yeah, there's one over near New Bremen. It's a hike and I ain't ridin' back wet on no motorcycle, even in this heat. We'll have to take my rig. I'm game if you are. It's a great place. We could pack a lunch and go after we get coffee'd up."

"Let's do it," Paul said emerging from the bathroom and drying off his face.

The two head off in Jolinda's pickup. Both windows are open and the hot air blowing in does little more that evaporate perspiration.

"I ain't been there in a 'coon's age. I remember where it is, but it'll take me a few minutes when we get to the mountain. I know I'll recognize it when I see it. It's a great place. You park on the side of the road and hike down a path through some ferns and then, there it is. It's a big stone basin with a waterfall flowing into it from above. The locals call it 'the tub'. If I remember right, it never really warms up like a slow-moving creek does. You can dive from the top of the waterfall, but gotta be careful to hit exactly where the water does, 'cause that's the only place where it's deep enough. I've never done it. I love to swim, but I'm not much on high diving. It's fun to watch the local hayseed boys showin' off for their girlfriends below who all pretend to be scared and 'ooh' and 'aah' and shout up to them to be careful. Then they all scream when the boy dives and yell and cheer when his head pops up out of the waterfall. They love that stuff. I suppose that's what you do until you can have real sex like you and me."

Paul looks embarrassed by her candor and then grins, grateful again that the woman driving next to him likes him and says so.

It's only an hour later and the two are driving home. They are still hot. Jolinda found the place but neither could bring themselves to swim.

To Jolinda's surprise, there is only one parked car.

"We're in luck," she says, turning to Paul. "I can't believe it, there's usually a dozen cars here on a hot day like today. Maybe we're early. It's only 11."

Paul looks up at the hill from which the creek tumbles down and says, "Someday, I'll show you a mountain. Back home, we'd call this a woodchuck mound."

Jolinda turns to him and radiates a smirk.

The two walk down the path, the beginning of which Jolinda finds with ease.

Sitting on a gravel rim of the basin two girls in bikinis sit holding each other. It's evident that they are crying. No one is swimming.

Jolinda looks at Paul quizzically as they approach the girls. She asks, "Where's everyone on a scorcher like today?"

One girl looks up and then looks down again, sobbing. The other looks up, tries to clear her throat and tells them that a boy just got hurt diving off the cliff, that he was taken by ambulance to the hospital and that all the other kids followed him there. The two girls didn't know the boy, but saw the accident happen and seemed anxious to describe it to Paul and Jolinda, the first newcomers on the scene.

"It was his first dive and the other boys was urgin' him to try it. He seemed nervous, but all the girls was watchin' down below and the boys was tellin' him how much fun it was and all, so finally he just took a step back and ran into a dive with his arms at his side. I never seen anyone dive like that, but he did. It looked like he slipped on the wet moss up there and kinda tripped off the edge. He musta landed in the shallow over there 'cause he din' even come close to the waterfall place where you're supposed to hit. Ain't more'n a few feet deep down where the ledge comes. He just floated to the surface. You could see his head was at a weird angle and he wasn't movin' or anything. The girls didn't do nothing but just scream and the boys rushed over to get him. It was a half hour before an ambulance came, 'cause, well, you prob'ly saw, the nearest farmhouse is a couple miles back and they musta had a phone. When help finally came, I think he was dead, but I ain' no doctor. Even though I don't know him, I don't want to know. It felt to us kinda like someone should stay here and tell folks in case they didn't want to swim where someone just died."

Paul and Jolinda just stared at the girl.

"Jolinda said to Paul, "Go ahead in, she's right. I can't do it.""

"Me, neither," said Paul and the two headed back up the path, leaving the two girls to keep watch over the scene where only the sound of falling water remained.

"I know a creek not far, shall we cool off there?"

Jolinda pulled over and bought a six pack of Rolling Rock and some chips to go with their sandwiches.

That night, lying in bed, Paul wondered out loud to Jolinda if the boy had survived.

"From what that poor girl said, I'm not sure I'd want to if I was him," said Jolinda.

After three weeks, Dr. Abrams believes Paul to be stable and improving. There is disturbing cognitive dissonance between Paul's anxiety about his wracked body, the claustrophobic terrors he experiences at night and Dr. Abrams' medical prognosis for him. The rotation of nurses who attend him twice daily record a continuum of positive notations on the clipboard hanging at the foot of his bed.

It's late in the afternoon. An orderly has just lifted him so a nurse can apply ointment to the proliferation of bedsores breaking out on the pressure points of his body on the mattress. The breaks in his skeleton preclude any changes in the traction that has immobilized him since his first surgery. Dr. Abrams worries about the remaining orthopedic repairs in his arm and hands. When Paul was brought in off the road and entered surgery, Dr. Abrams and his trauma team worked only to save Paul's life, leaving non-lethal damage for later surgeries. The work of stabilizing Paul is done and Dr. Abrams has scheduled additional tests and surgeries he plans to discuss with Paul.

The familiar and nauseous smell of evening meal distribution pervades his room, indicating to him that the door has opened, and he waits for the orderly bearing his unappetizing tray to begin coaxing supper into him. He is surprised, however, to see his father in front of him holding a bowl of fresh-picked Macs from the orchard in the high meadow above the farm. Paul's father is uncomfortable and does not look at his son directly.

His father has never visited him alone before and both feel awkward. Paul knows his father to be a practical man. By his nature, he will assess his son's chances of future utility. He knows, too, that he is a kind man, not without a deep well of feeling for his family. Paul imagines his father looking at a piece of wrecked farm equipment, the kind often left to rust away in fallow fields, and having to make a practical decision as to whether or not it can ever be made to function again. Paul looks into his father's eyes, but they are hidden by heavy gray eyelashes that prevent Paul from seeing what his father sees.

His father places the bowl of apples on the bedside table and declines the chair Paul points to with his one functioning hand.

"I can't stay long," *his father opens.* "Mother is alone at home and it's supposed to go below freezing tonight. She wanted to come, but it's hard for us both to make the drive except on Sunday when I can get Luther or Tommy to help with the milking."

"Is Tommy back? Is he okay?" *Paul asks.*

"He's back; can't say he's okay. Folks have kinda shunned him, ya know. He's pretty open about being a homosexual and that scares people. He don't bother anyone, though, keeps to himself and gets odd jobs from the folks who can tolerate him. Ma and I let him live up at Theron's, least 'til you get home."

His father looks away, fearing that he has misspoken in assuming that his son could ever live at Theron's in this condition. There is a long silence. An orderly enters and quietly sets a gray, rectangular, sectional-molded plastic tray of grayish meat and vegetables on the window sill. The orderly assumes that the patient's visitor will relieve him of the need to spoon the food into her charge's mouth.

"Help yourself, Dad, I just can't eat that stuff," *Paul offers with a faint smile.*

"Not like mom's cooking that's for sure."

"You have to eat, son. You need food to get well."

"I'll take one of those apples. Can you slice it up? There's a knife wrapped in that napkin on the food tray," Paul says. But his father reaches into his pocket and pulls out his familiar Case Trapper pocket knife.

When Paul was eight, his father gave him the smaller model of the same knife for his birthday. It was Paul's most valued possession until, fishing with Tommy in Long Pond, he lost it. He cried himself to sleep for several nights until Glenda suggested that they return to the fishing site to look for it. They didn't find it, though.

Several days later as Glenda opened the mailbox at the end of their road after the two had stepped off the school bus, she saw it lying there with a hastily scrawled note from Tommy, who said that he had "slipped the knife into his creel by mistake when Tommy left it on a rock where he was gutting the German brown he caught." Paul was overjoyed. His anger at his friend dissolved during the walk to the house as he and Glenda talked of the untold deprivations that might have motivated his friend to steal the knife or "borrow it," as she suggested might have been the case.

Paul's father extends a slice of apple on the end of the knife toward Paul who draws it off the knife's tip with his teeth. The juice from the apple shoots neural lightning into his jaw and he cringes at the familiar pain, and the pleasure of a crisp new Mac.

"As good as I remember them ...," he says to his father, whom he catches looking into his eyes for the first time.

"Dad, I'm sorry about college. I know how much you and mom wanted this for me and I tried. Remember how hard you told me it was when you were in high school and how your mind kept drifting away to other things. Well, I got through high school, but not college. I'm not like Glenda. I'd daydream and then fret over how I'd get through three more years. I'd think of the farm and home and the lake and think about what I wanted to do. I'd imagine how I was going to earn a living, eventually buy the land, and fix up Uncle Theron's cabin into a nice place to raise a family. I thought about selling

firewood and maybe doing some trapping or being a hunting and fishing guide on the lake. Everything I was learning in college prepared me for a job sitting indoors and I knew I couldn't do that. I need to be outdoors just like you said you did."

His father looks away and then slices off another piece of apple for his son.

"Does it hurt much?" his father asks. "I mean all that rigging ..."

"I can't feel a lot below my waist. It's the bedsores that hurt and itch and I get a sort of panic at night at not being able to move out of this position. There are itches I can't reach and I don't really know what is happening or how they plan to fix me, if they can," Paul answers while savoring the apple slice.

"I wish we were haying," he adds, "must be second cutting."

Paul likes working as a laborer. His work assignments change every few days, if not daily. He has seen how a house is built from the footings up through the interior finish. Though he has not done every task, he has been assigned to assist tradesmen doing most aspects of house construction. The site boss has rewarded his consistent hard work and punctuality by occasionally allowing him to help the subcontracted plumbers and electricians when they were short-handed.

Paul observes as a plumber burnishes the male copper fitting with emery cloth, then brushes it with a Vaseline-like flux, fits it into the female joint, rotates it into place, and then heats the male end with a hand torch until the solder suddenly melts and flows deep into the joint.

Paul drills conduit courses through upright studs and feeds 14-gauge wire through the holes from switch boxes to fixture boxes and to outlets. He learns to read circuit drawings and to select three-conductor wire or four-conductor wire, depending on the switching layout. The electricians won't let him make any wire connections for fear of an inspector's citing a mistake, but seem to enjoy his attention to their work and indulge his occasional questions.

He watches finish carpenters rough-in counter tops and cabinets, framing spaces for dishwashers, washing machines, stoves and refrigerators. He learns to measure and cut the 4 x 8 sheetrock to cover over the wiring and plumbing within the studwork.

Sabin, whom the workers seem to delight in calling *Frenchie, the shitrocker*, speaks little English, but takes the time to show Paul how to apply the "mud" over the joints and nail dimples with a large rectangular trowel and the next day to sand it smooth with a block and sandpaper and then to reapply more mud until the sheetrock wall appears perfectly smooth and is ready for the off-white paint that Sabin's paint-spattered wife applies with her rollers. Only on the rare occasion when he thinks of his mother and father, does his failure in college come back to trouble him. He enjoys what he is learning on the jobsite and knows he will be able to use much of it when he returns home.

He looks forward to riding his new bike each evening back to Jolinda. Both are a continuing source of pleasure to him. He recalls the words of a song he has heard several times on the transistor radio that is always on near the picnic benches on the jobsite, "… a '52 Vincent and a red-headed girl …" and he remembers Danny's Vincent Black Shadow, but has to work harder to remember Danny.

He remembers as a child, wanting things like his own pocketknife, a .22 Winchester, a bamboo flyrod, or the double-bitted ax with its beautiful engraving on the axehead that Theron gave him. He knows now that desire peaks in the pleasure of getting and then subsides into utility. But Paul has not lost the thrill of starting and riding his new bike.

The responsiveness of the V-twin to a subtle inflection of his wrist on the throttle continues to thrill him. Perhaps it's the roar of the straight pipes or the joy of banking into a turn and applying more power as he emerges from the turn. The utility and economy of his first bike, on which he could never depend, has been replaced by the joy of riding the chopped panhead.

Jolinda is rarely home when he returns. The record store closes at six, but the evenings on which she clerks for her father are not regular, as they are determined by his caseload. She can usually tell Paul when she will be home.

Paul enjoys making a nice meal for Jolinda and having the table set and food ready for her when she arrives. He feels it is an appropriate way to thank her for letting him stay with her. He cannot remember his father ever preparing a meal for his mother, but his mother did not work outside the home other than to tend her flock of biddies and the small kitchen garden she maintained in the summer. Her volunteer duties at Grange were sporadic and never seemed to interfere with her homemaking. Paul is still unsure of why Jolinda has taken him in.

One day at work, Jerry is injured. He'd finished excavating a large hole for the massive septic tank that will service the housing development and has begun digging a radial web of trenches off the septic cavity to create a leach field for the gray water run-off. His work area is dangerously pocked with random piles of pea stone and sand deposited for use later in backfilling once the Orangeburg pipe is laid in and leveled. The sand and pea stone will enhance the leaching capacity of the mostly clay soil.

Jerry has been having trouble all morning with the tracks on his excavator and is kneeling by them greasing the rollers and expanding the tighteners on the tracks with a large box wrench. The idling excavator is parked parallel to the deep trough he has just finished digging when the dirt wall collapses and the rig falls sideways into the ditch. Jerry's left leg is pinned under the track he has been working on. He cries out in pain. Everyone nearby sees the accident happen and rallies quickly. Several nearby men rush to the site dragging tow chains that they attach to the upside of the excavator and to a 'dozer hoping to pull the excavator away from and off its victim but to no avail. The 'dozer with its own cleated tracks simply does not have the traction to move the larger excavator, and simply digs two holes in the soil beneath it with its own rotating tracks.

Jerry is conscious and in shock. Several men are by his side as he explains to them how to lift the tracks off his leg. One man volunteers to attempt the rescue and climbs into the excavator's cab which is at a precarious angle with one track much higher than the one pinning Jerry's leg. Jerry whispers directions to the man by his side who shouts them over the idling diesel to the man in the cab. Jerry explains that the operator will use the excavator's hydraulic arm to lift the cab and tracks off his leg.

After several minutes of trial and error, the novice operator soon gets the hang of the floor levers and how they manipulate the excavator arm. He moves the arm into place on the other side of the ditch in which Jerry is lying and sets the bucket down hard on firm soil. He then uses the hydraulics to life the cab slightly off Jerry's leg enough so that the men can drag him to safety. The huge weight of the tracks causes them to skew sideways before lifting off and Jerry faints from the pain.

An ambulance is waiting nearby and Jerry is handed onto a stretcher by several men. The ambulance leaves with its sirens howling into the distance from the now quiet worksite. The departure of the ambulance ends the event, but the men linger in silence. Some talk quietly and shake their heads, knowing that this could have happened to any of them

At quitting time, Paul finds out from the crew boss where they would have taken Jerry in hopes of visiting him, but he finds out that only family will be allowed in for the next few days and he will have to wait before he can see him. He learns from one of the ambulance EMTs that Jerry will almost certainly lose the injured leg.

The incident has cast a pall over the worksite that lasts for several days. The usual blare of competing transistor radios on the site is silenced and the joviality of the mid-morning and afternoon breaks is replaced by men talking quietly in small groups, smoking cigarettes, sipping milky coffee, and eating hard rolls with butter, or doughnuts from the snack truck that shows up at break times.

Paul goes home that evening. Jolinda arrives shortly after and suggests they go out for a beer and burgers. Paul agrees, recognizing that neither has the stamina or appetite to prepare food for the other. Paul recounts the accident; Jolinda remembers Jerry from the VFW dance and barbecue.

With little reaction to Paul's news, Jolinda begins to lay out her doubts about becoming a lawyer. She likes working in the record shop, especially when there are no customers and she can listen over and over again to her favorite records while committing to memory the melodies and lyrics. She knows it's a dead-end job, yet any teen in town would nab it for the 20 percent discount on records. She also knows if she retires in the job, she'll still be making the equivalent of $3 an hour.

The work with her father is boring. His cases are mostly real estate and trust transactions, and the menial work that he assigns her holds no interest beyond its possible gossip value in the community, but Jolinda is not a gossip and looks down on people who are. Neither is she sure she's learning enough to pass the Ohio bar exam. Word has it in the legal community that the tradition of clerking for the law may end soon, and Jolinda does not have the wherewithal to pay for law school. If her father cosigned loans, she could borrow the money, but she has managed her life so far without debt and is loath to assume any.

Jolinda's one passion is music and she knows from her performing friends that home life and family relationships are always casualties of the profession. She has been asked several times to join the band she accompanied at the picnic as a lead vocalist and has been asked to join other old-timey, bluegrass and country groups, but has, until now, kept her sights on the practice of law. The drudgery of document analysis and exchange, however, has diminished her enthusiasm for the practice of law.

The disheartening topics lead Jolinda to suggest they return home. Paul sheds his work clothes and goes to the shower. Jolinda joins him in the small shower. Although the warmth of water falling from the showerhead, the proximity of one another's flesh, and the security of being held have been the inevitable preludes to lovemaking, Jolinda simply holds Paul tightly against herself under the warm shower and cries quietly. Paul asks if she is okay. She doesn't answer. They hold each other under the warm rush of water until Jolinda eventually loosens her grip on Paul and emerges from the shower stall. Paul continues lathering and rinsing himself and then shaves. When he pulls back the curtain Jolinda is gone. He finds her in bed under the covers and facing away from him. He gets into bed and holds her to himself. She is still damp and warm. She doesn't resist, being held and the two fall asleep.

Dr. Abrams is explaining the sequence that Paul's body will endure during what is expected to be a five-hour operation. The doctor's demeanor is without affect and his monotone baritone betrays no emotion or empathy. He tells Paul that when he wakes up, he will be in a partial body cast for a three-month convalescence while his pelvis knits. He will be out of traction, but will still require help changing his position in bed because of the weight of the cast and the atrophy in his muscles. Dr. Abrams drones on, explaining that he will have a better sense of the damage to Paul's spine and his future prospects for mobility after the neurology tests and surgery.

Paul's attention drifts and Dr. Abrams' voice recedes. Paul closes his eyes and is back in college in Mr. Cedron's course called The English Novel. Mr. Cedron is prating on enthusiastically about how Jude the Obscure reflects the stultifying class-segmentation of life in 19th century England. Paul didn't finish the book and failed the first two quizzes. Mr. Cedron, too, has consigned Paul to failure and reflects this in his grade for the semester. Paul is indifferent and spends much of Mr. Cedron's class recalling and inhabiting the landscape of his home with Glenda, Tommy, and Theron.

Paul's mind returns to the hospital room only when Dr. Abrams asks him in a louder voice if he has any questions about the surgery. Paul must say "no" out loud, as Dr. Abrams is staring intently at his chart and would not see him nod. Paul is unable to muster any attention to the details of his medical care.

Dr. Abrams leaves and Paul is again alone. A beige Princess phone has been placed within his reach. He has never seen such a phone. He is used to the large black Bakelite dial phone at the farm or the coin phones at college. He wants to talk to Glenda but the expense of an international call intimidates him. He succumbs to his loneliness. He thinks of his thwarted plans to move into Theron's and to fix up the cabin. He is overwhelmed with an urge to run, drive, fish, and dive into the lake and swim for miles, but also to talk with his sister.

He dials the number in his head, but halfway through finds he is unsure of the sequence of the last four digits. He tries what he believes to be the most intuitive sequence. He hears relays clicking and then ringing. A man's voice answers in French. Paul knows there would be no such voice in the dorm in which Glenda lives and hangs up.

His desperation manifests itself in an effort to stand up and walk away from his hospital bed. There is no response, however, to the shriek of neural transmissions from his brain other than a twitch in his legs. His head falls back on the pillow.

Later, he is awakened by the sound of a bicycle bell. It is coming from within the new phone, the first time the small phone has ever rung. He is surprised by the similarity of its ring to that heard coming from a bicycle. It is Glenda. He looks at the wall clock. It is 9:25 p.m. and he cannot remember if he has been given his sleeping pill. The sleep has allayed his anxiety, but not his hopelessness. He is trying to remember what it was that he wanted Glenda's help with. Or did he simply want to hear her voice?

Glenda's voice is calming, though he is haunted by the knowledge that he needed her for something he cannot remember. Was it to help him leave and go to Theron's? Was it to take him to Long Pond for a swim? He is content now just to hear her voice.

Glenda tells him that their mother's diabetes has worsened and she is again on insulin and must monitor her blood sugar levels. The price of milk is down again and milking 35 cows no longer provides a living for their parents. The need and desire to be home again wells up in Paul.

While Glenda is talking to him, he interrupts her and says, "Sis, I can't do this. I get so scared in the middle of the night. I can't move. I felt trapped in college but I could simply walk away. Now, I can't walk anywhere. No one has told me I will ever walk anywhere again. I'm so scared."

The phone is silent. Glenda tells him that Canadian Thanksgiving is coming the following week and that she will come home and be with him for the three-day holiday.

Paul is relieved by this, though he does not know what changes are within Glenda's power, other than the joy her presence brings to him.

The move from his hospital bed onto a gurney for transport to neurology discharges cannon shots of pain.

He is being wheeled down a long corridor in a remote corner of the hospital. During the nerve conduction tests, Paul is conscious so he can respond to questions that help the neurologist analyze the extent of damage to his spinal cord. A series of electrical stimuli is applied to Paul's body through needles at different points. Paul is asked to identify the precise location of what he feels—or whether he feels anything at all.

He endures the nerve conduction tests easily enough. The induced neural tingling he can feel reminds him of what he used to feel when a limb fell asleep. Occasionally, the electrical impulses elicit painful muscle spasms but he doesn't feel many of the stimuli and shakes his head sideways to the nurse taking notes.

An hour later in the surgical suite, he is again looking up into the face of Dr. Abrams, whom he can recognize now only by the deep voice coming from behind a surgical mask and the heavy-set, black-frame glasses. The blinding light hurts Paul's eye and he feels a headache rising in his temples. The last thing he hears is a nurse telling him they are going to put him under as he notices a nurse inserting a needle into his IV line. Within the same minute, there is only the cessation of consciousness. He will remember only the image of the nurse putting the needle into the blue T-joint on a tube leading to his wrist.

Paul wakes, hearing Jolinda in the kitchen making coffee. He smells toast. It is 6:15 and he must be at work now at 7. The days are getting shorter and the crew now works from 7 to 3:30 p.m. with a half-hour lunch break. He joins Jolinda who is still quiet. She smiles at him and offers him a warm "good morning." The two quietly eat their breakfast of eggs over easy on toast with coffee.

"I'll be gone this weekend," Jolinda says looking at him. "The band asked me to front for them at the Montgomery County Fair outside of Dayton and I agreed. I need to make this music thing work and it ain't gonna be shuffling paper in my dad's office when he retires."

Paul looks at Jolinda.

"That's good news," he says. "Want me to come with you? We could take your truck."

"No, I need to be alone and think. You make me too comfortable when I'm with you. I love being with you. I love you ...," she says, looking away with what appears to Paul to be sadness.

"Is that a bad thing?" Paul asks. "I love you, too," he adds, fearing suddenly that he has just expressed himself in an inconsequential way, as if he were asking her to lend him lunch money. This is not how he had imagined telling a woman he loved her. He is ashamed of himself.

Jolinda looks at him and smiles, "I know you do," she says, "And I love you dearly, maybe more than you can ever feel, but ...."

Jolinda's voice trails off.

"But what?" asks Paul.

"But nothing," Jolinda smiles enigmatically, suppressing his inquiry. "I love you."

Jolinda gives him a sudden kiss, puts their dishes in the sink and says, "See you this evening. We'll have fun."

Paul rides to work with a lingering sense of malaise about their conversation. He meant to tell Jo that he was going to visit Jerry that evening and would be home an hour later than usual, but with the earlier quitting hours, he will be able to visit Jerry and still be home before Jolinda.

Paul spends the day helping a sub lay asphalt floor tile in two kitchens. He is pleased with all that he learns about measuring the floor, finding its center point, and beginning to lay the tile from the center point out toward the kitchen's perimeter. He had assumed one would start flush along one wall and lay the tiles across the floor's expanse to the other side, trimming only those tiles that did not fit. But the tiler, Kenny, takes the time to show him the resulting asymmetry.

Kenny shows him how to trowel on the adhesive with the corrugated edge of his rectangular trowel and then to lay the tiles onto the furrowed adhesive only after it is tacky enough to adhere, yet still fresh enough to snug the tiles up tight to the row he just set.

At break, he hears that Jerry has indeed lost his leg and will be on disability for the rest of his life. Paul is surprised at the conversation among his peers that seems to favor the idea that Jerry has gotten a good deal, as he will never again have to work if he doesn't want to, and can live out his life fishing or indulging whatever leisure activity he chooses. An older framing carpenter observes, however, that it is a terrible price to pay for early retirement.

Paul has been feeling guilty because no one in his family knows how to reach him in an emergency. He resolves to call Glenda and to tell her his number at Jolinda's in case she or his parents need to reach him. He has been avoiding telling Glenda about Jolinda. Though he does not fully understand why, he worries that Glenda might feel his affection for Jolinda will diminish his love of her.

Paul rides to the hospital in Defiance. There he learns that Jerry is in the psychiatric ward and can only see family members. Paul uses the visitor phone in the waiting area to call Glenda. He has sixteen quarters in his pocket. After a three-quarter wait, Glenda picks up the phone. She scolds him mildly for being so out of touch, but finishes by telling him how glad she is to hear his voice.

Glenda fills the space between them with talk of home, new economic hardships on the farm, and the minor health problems suffered by their parents. She then asks about his news. He tells Glenda about Jerry's accident and how much he is learning at work. He tells her enthusiastically about his new bike and promises her a ride when he gets home for Thanksgiving.

She asks if he is still at Mrs. Benton's and he answers only that he has moved to cheaper lodging. He adds that he and Mrs. Benton are keeping up their friendship. He is not ready to talk about Jolinda and, in any case, would want it to be a longer conversation than he has quarters for. He asks coyly if she has a boyfriend yet. Glenda answers demurely that she is seeing a boy from Toronto, though she insists they are not "going together." Paul leaves Glenda with Jolinda's number in case of emergency and a promise to be home for Thanksgiving.

When he returns to the apartment, Jolinda is not yet home. Paul showers and warms up some leftovers in the toaster oven. He drops onto the couch and lets his fatigue wash over him. The smell of burning meatloaf and potato wakes him and he runs into the kitchen where the smoky residue of their meal hangs visibly in the air. He opens the window over the sink and an unused backdoor to a makeshift fire escape. There's enough breeze outside to draw off the bluish smoke, but the smell lingers.

Paul drops back down on the couch and is soon asleep.

Jolinda wakes him just before midnight with a kiss. Her breath exudes the smell of beer. She teases Paul into bed where she has perfunctory sex with him. Afterwards, she rolls off him and falls asleep, snoring softly.

Paul is wide awake now and the lingering smell of beer makes him thirsty. He gets quietly out of bed for a glass of water and returns, afraid that he will never get back to sleep. Lying on his side, he looks at the woman lying next to him. She, too, is lying on her side and the moist exhalations coming from between her lips warm his forearm; her inhalations are soft sinusoidal flutters that are less than snoring. He notices the faintest trace of blond hair in the gentle furrows of her upper lip. A slight septal concavity defines a pert and smallish nose that enhances her intermittent smile belying an active dream state.

Paul looks closely at the wisps of hazel hair arrayed on her right temple and cheek and brushes them gently from her eyes. He notices that her eyelids, too, are enlisted neurally in her dreams.

He loves to look at Jolinda's breasts while she is sleeping. He's alone in a world wherein he can enjoy their beauty without feeling self-conscious about paying such close and enduring attention. He recalls his futile boyhood efforts to imagine the breasts of girls he saw; the only hint of their beguiling beauty the subtle or prominent rise beneath a dress or sweater. He was alone in bed with a sleeping woman who was happy to have him see, admire, and caress her breasts with his eyes, hands and lips. He vacillates between doing so and possibly waking her again and just enjoying the frisson of admiring her in a dream state.

Jolinda inhales deeply and rolls over leaving Paul to see the tanned nape of her neck, the soft blades of her shoulders, and the disarray of dark hair on her white pillow. His eyes follow the rippled ridgeline of her back descending into the declivity of her kidneys, the abrupt symmetry of her buttocks, and the mysterious cleft that disappears between the backs of her thighs.

He, too, rolls onto his back and suddenly recalls his conversation with Glenda. He tries to imagine her with a boyfriend. He wonders uncomfortably if they have sex, though he doubts they do, as Glenda always said on the rare occasions they talked about it when they were younger, that she would only make love with her husband. He wonders if she will change her mind. The subject makes him uncomfortable and his reveries shift to his mother and father's troubles on the farm.

He realizes that his parents are getting on, and that, in their absence and in his imagination, they have retained the age and vitality of his childhood. He worries about his mother's diabetes. He remembers Tommy's grandmother dying of "the sugar" when she was 48. His father's arthritic hips and knees will eventually preclude his twice daily milking, mucking out gutters, fixing fence, and hauling bales around the barn.

Paul wonders how Tommy is getting on at Theron's cabin. He knows Tommy to be resourceful, but Theron's cabin is so sparse as to require almost full time work to live there year around. He wonders if Tommy will ever find someone to love him, and how, and whether that person will be a boy or a girl.

He remembers his last hike up Mount Wheeler with Tommy, an easy climb, less than an hour if they keep at it. Paul has been looking for ways to distract Tommy from his mounting troubles at home. Tommy, who is usually a spigot of observations and curiosity, is uncharacteristically quiet. The two climb steadily, Paul tries to engage his friend in conversation, but Tommy responds mostly in monosyllables or with grunting acknowledgments.

Paul invites his friend to set the pace and lead for a while, but Tommy says he would rather follow Paul up the narrow trail. His silence begins to make Paul uncomfortable.

They stop near the top where a small rill traverses the path. It is barely deep enough to ladle out a handful of water with two hands. The two drink several handfuls of water and Paul heads off toward the summit.

"I'm gonna stay here for a bit. I'll be along shortly," says Tommy. A warm breeze carries his words quickly off the mountainside.

"I can wait for you if you wanna rest for a bit," Paul assures him.

"No, you go on ahead. I'll be along in a few minutes. I'm okay," Tommy answers. Unsure, Paul heads up the thinning trail.

Though Mount Wheeler is lower than its massive neighbors, Mount Pisgah and Mount Hor, the climbers will see the pair in their full drama from Wheeler's summit with the deep blue gash of Lake Willoughby lying between their cliffs. It is this view that the two climb up to see.

Paul reaches the top in fifteen minutes and sits down on the crag facing the lake. He and Tommy and Glenda have walked up through the mountain's covert of ancient sugar maples countless times to enjoy this view.

Looking down the back side of Mount Hor, Paul can see three chicken hawks circling in wide arcs high above the meadow between the base of Mount Wheeler and Tommy's farmhouse nearby. Paul's farm is not visible from the top, as it lies on the backside of Mount Pisgah and in the shadow of Pisgah's bald rock summit. He waits another twenty minutes for his friend and then heads back down the trail to meet him and offer encouragement, but he does not find Tommy anywhere on the trail back to the brook. Nor is his friend at the brook.

Paul calls out for Tommy several times, cupping his hands around his mouth to amplify his voice as Theron has taught him, but there is no response. He hears nothing but the breeze in the leaves above and the lone trill of a phoebe. He puts his index and middle fingers on his lower lip and manages a shrill wolf whistle into the quiet woods around him, but again there is no response. He and Tommy have agreed since they were little to use this whistle if one or the other gets lost or separated when they are camping or fishing. Again, there is no response.

Paul stops at the farmhouse when he reaches the bottom, but Tommy's father says gruffly that Tommy hasn't been there and that his mother is in town trading for goods before he closes the door. Paul smells liquor.

For several days, Paul remains puzzled by his friend's disappearance. It is unlike Tommy to simply disappear. Paul doesn't see Tommy for several days and then one day, breathless, Tommy rides up to Paul's house on his bike and suggests the two go for a swim at the south end of the lake.

While the two are swimming in choppy waters twenty feet above South Beach's white sand bottom, Paul asks Tommy where he went when they were climbing.

"I was beating off," Tommy answers. Paul doesn't react and the two continue their swim.

Paul is lying quietly next to Jolinda and again tries to make sense of his friend's comment in the light of his admitted homosexuality.

Paul again hears Jolinda making coffee in the kitchen. He is aware that he has not slept anywhere near his usual seven hours, though he cannot remember when that morning he fell asleep. He guesses he has had four or five hours of sleep and knows he will be tired well before his work day ends. Being tired doesn't trouble him as much as the lack of acuity and attention he experiences, especially when he is learning new skills and focusing on getting a task done properly. He knows some others on the crew have a more slapdash attitude about their work, but he finds that learning something new and doing it well compensate for the feelings of inadequacy he felt in college.

Jolinda forgoes breakfast and Paul has toast and peanut butter with his coffee.

"I'll be back late Sunday night after the second set. Why don't you go have a nice Sunday dinner with Mrs. Benton? I'm sure she'd love to see you," she says looking up from her coffee. "I just don't wanna hear you two have been gettin' it on, ya hear?"

"No worries on that score, I promise," says Paul with an involuntary smile.

"Take care and have fun. I'll be home soon."

Jo leaves, and he hears her rapid steps retreating down the stairs and out the front door.

Paul rinses out his mug and plate and leaves them dripping in the drying rack.

"Paul, can you hear me? Paul, you're in the recovery room. We finished the operation in a little under six hours. You did very well. We're going to let you rest for a while and then I'll come see you. We're going to keep you here until tomorrow where they can monitor your pain more closely. Do you feel any pain now? "

Paul thinks to himself, "How did _I_ do well? He must mean he did well. I didn't do anything."

Paul can think, but doesn't respond to the familiar baritone. He doesn't feel any pain, but he can't communicate that. Dr. Sametz seems satisfied that his patient is not in pain and leaves, addressing himself to the nurse who follows him out.

Sixteen hours have elapsed and Paul again hears the familiar voice, "Paul, I need your full attention."

Dr. Abrams and Dr. Sametz are looking down on Paul, but this time Dr. Sametz is wearing a white coat instead of scrubs and there is no mask over his face, only the glasses, which he removes and polishes with a tissue he draws from the box by Paul's bed.

Paul thinks he can see his mother, father and Glenda standing near the entrance to the recovery room.

"Paul, I have some good news and some not so good news to tell you. As I told you yesterday the surgery went well. We have repaired most of the damage to your arm and ribs. You will need additional surgery on your right hand that can come later and perhaps some skin graft work. You will not, however, walk again. The nerve damage within your spinal cord is not something we yet know enough to repair. You have paraplegia and will be wheelchair-bound. I have asked a counselor to come and talk you through the implications of living a life as a paraplegic. It is not all bad news. We have made many advances that will make the rest of your life very manageable and productive. Do you have any questions? If not, I will leave you with your family."

After a brief pause, the doctors turn and leave the room, nodding to Paul's family that they can now approach their son and confront his reaction, even *as they are still trying to process their own. Paul's father, mother and sister were briefed on the diagnosis beforehand and on how the bad news will be delivered. A counselor has answered their non-medical questions and made suggestions as to how they can best "be there" for Paul as he "processes" this news.*

Glenda disregards the counselor's admonition and sobs openly when Paul looks to his sister.

Paul catnaps during the fifteen-minute afternoon break. He chooses a spot on the periphery of the jobsite and lies down in the uncut grass with his arms under his head. He does not fall asleep but daydreams under an overcast sky. The brief respite restores him, and when he returns to his work setting and leveling new appliances in place and watching how the plumbers and electricians connect them up, he feels a surge of enthusiasm and affection and decides to surprise Jolinda by turning up for her performance at the county fair on Saturday.

A look at his wrinkled Ohio map indicates it's about 130 miles. Paul will give himself three hours to make the trip, though much of it will be on the Interstate. He vows to get a good night's rest and does so, falling asleep shortly after 9:30 p.m. and sleeping soundly until 5:30.

After a breakfast of peanut butter and toast with leftover strips of bacon and two cups of strong coffee, Paul spends an hour straightening up the apartment. He washes and puts away several days' worth of dishes, wipes down the kitchen surfaces and straightens up the living room where, under the ring-stained birch coffee table, he finds a cache of *Hustler* magazines. He has seen a few glossy *Playboy* centerfolds, but has never encountered the anatomical intimacy of this magazine, the covers of which he has only seen in gas stations and in some newsstands.

He pages through the images of intra-labial flesh, but his discomfort with the magazines and the fetishist candor in the graphic ads troubles him and he returns them to their place beneath a pile of country music magazines. He's always known that he is not Jolinda's first lover, though she was his, but he is surprised that some prior lover's porn stash remains behind.

Paul leaves around nine. The day is again overcast, but blades of sunshine occasionally permeate the cloud cover. He has never traveled on the new Interstate before. The unbroken asphalt surface and the choice of two travel lanes allow him the rare opportunity to shift into fifth and open the throttle. He is careful to travel at the speed of traffic, which he judges to be about 70 miles an hour. There are no instruments on his bike or any fuel gauge on the tank. Paul uses the universal hand signals to change lanes that he learned when he first got his learner's permit in Vermont at fifteen, though he had been driving farm vehicles on the dirt roads around Westmore since he was twelve.

Interstate 75 is a more or less straight incision through the flat and rolling farm country, and the familiar smells of fallow and cropped fields come back to him in the open air. He passes a hitchhiker illegally seeking a ride south near the exit for Lima, but does not want the joy of his ride diminished by a passenger.

He exits in Piqua to check his gas and finds the teardrop tank almost empty. He refills it, hands the cashier three ones, pockets coin change, and leaves again, back up the ramp and onto the highway.

Coming into Dayton, he sees a billboard advertising the Montgomery County Fair at Exit 51. Descending the ramp and following the directions, he has no trouble spotting the fairgrounds with its Ferris wheel looming on the horizon. He pulls in, pays for a day admission, and enters a vast parking lot in a closely-mowed hayfield. He hopes there is a lot for motorcycles where his bike will be less conspicuous, but he sees bikes intermingled with pickups, RVs, and cars throughout the parking lot. He parks between a camper and a jeep, removes the keys, and locks the fuel tank, not so much for fear of his gas being siphoned for there is too little in the teardrop tank to make it worth anyone's while, but because Hilger warned him that some people associate choppers with gangs and they'll empty a packet of sugar into the gas tank to destroy the engine. Hilger gave him a locking gas cap.

It's 1:30 and he has time to kill before the concert stage opens at 8. Paul has always relished county fairs and never missed the Barton and Caledonia County fairs at home.

As he walks around the exhibition tents, he is at first surprised by the relative lack of livestock and the plethora of consumer products offered. There are booths touting miracle roofing with a lifetime guarantee, skin lotions, vinyl siding, vitamin supplements, appliances, exercise equipment, and water softening and purification devices.

He leaves this tent and wanders over to the farm equipment area, crowded with shiny new tractors, combines, balers, corn choppers and the like. He recognizes all the equipment, but is astounded by the size of the combines. These he has seen only in farm magazine pictures, several at a time in formation, harvesting wheat in flat fields with no horizons. There is little use for a combine of this size on the hill farms in Westmore.

The largest tractors in the 140-HP-and-up class, too, are a novelty to him. He climbs aboard one and is struck by the almost living room-like characteristics of its temperature-controlled cab and spring-loaded seat. Power steering, hydrostatic shifting, AM-FM radio, and hydraulic brakes are all new to him. He is used to his father's 50-horse 2240 John Deere diesel with its battered front bucket and cranky differential. Paul climbs from cab to cab, inspecting the novel features of the new tractors.

After leaving the farm equipment area, he wanders over to the stock arena where the antique tractor pulls are in progress. He had been hearing the roar of diesel and gasoline engines, but had not connected them with the pulls. Leaning on the white perimeter fence, he watches a Massey-Harris with its deep-treaded balloon tires hauling a weight transfer sledge piled high with concrete blocks the size of coffins down the 300-foot track. As the tractor progresses and the drag increases, it bucks up on its hind wheels and the front axle bobs in the air as it struggles, adding its own weight to the torque needed to move the load attached to its drawbar.

The Massey-Harris completes the haul and is followed by an Oliver 1850, a Minneapolis Moline, and then a John Deere 4455, which does not make it to the end of the course. The tractors, belching black smoke and roaring at or near their redlines, draw loud cheers from the crowd.

Paul watches the last of the tractors in this class and then heads off into the array of stock barns. Inside, he sees breeds and some animals that are new to him: llamas, alpacas, Nubian goats, Angora sheep, and a pair of black swans hissing at the spectators who approach their pen. He loves seeing the exotics, and in the next tent encounters a number of unfamiliar beef breeds including Charolais, Belgian Blues, Short Horns, and Brahmans. At home, few farmers raise beef other than for their own use so familiar cows are mostly Holstein, Guernsey, Jersey and the occasional Brown Swiss.

He's thirsty and stops by a stand selling fresh-squeezed lemonade. He points to the tall cup and watches as the smiling young woman's hand presses the juice of three lemons into a cup full of crushed ice, adds a dash of water and two tablespoons of sugar. She attaches the lid, shakes the cup vigorously while smiling at him, and then forces a straw through the punch-in in the top, and hands it to him.

"$1.25," she says, "You from around here?"

"No, from Vermont," Paul says.

"Long way to come for a fair, ain't it?" she asks, beaming.

"Well, I been working up near Defiance ... summer job," Paul answers, turning away.

"Come back if you get thirsty again," the young woman yells after him.

"I will," he says.

Unexpectedly, Jolinda walks out of the children's pony ride tent. She is holding the right hand of a little girl about six or seven years old. A larger woman, wearing a suede leather jacket with fringe, holds the girl's other hand.

Paul is about to bolt forward and greet Jolinda, but the expression on her face when she turns to address what he assumes is the girl's mother dissuades him abruptly. He follows the three for a ways, hanging back in the crowd. Jolinda begins laughing hard at something the mother says and leans over the little girl to kiss the other woman and then winks broadly. Paul senses an intimacy beyond friendship, but then worries that he is misreading what he sees. Could Jolinda be the little girl's aunt?

Jo has never spoken to Paul of a sister or a niece. In fact she has given the distinct impression of being her father's only child. The girl runs ahead toward the merry-go-round, pointing at the ride and looking back plaintively to the two women with her, making clear her desire to ride on an outer horse.

Jolinda buys a ticket from the carnie standing at the gate and the other woman hoists the girl onto a palomino in full frozen gait on the vertical chrome post. The girl is grinning broadly and wraps both her small hands around the chrome pole in anticipation. The canned hurdy-gurdy music begins and the platform slowly begins to rotate, as the same carnie who sold them the ticket draws back on a large clutch lever in the inner radius of the merry-go-round where an open V-6 engine chugs away under a spinning throttle governor in a small cloud of exhaust.

As the ride comes up to speed, the little girl's face tightens along with her grasp on the pole and the two women wave at her through several rotations. Jolinda then radiates a broad smile at her friend, throws her arms around her neck and kisses her on the lips.

At first, Paul is confused. He gets a better look at the woman and sees there is no family resemblance. She appears slightly older than Jolinda, perhaps in her early thirties. He is closer than he wants to be, but he is out of their view near an adjacent tent. Suddenly he is ashamed that he is spying on Jolinda and decides to go up and greet her, but then loses courage and walks away.

He recalls Hilger's allusion to "that bitch," and begins to wonder if Jolinda, in fact, has or had a girlfriend. He leaves the area where they are and goes back to the familiar safety of the stock shed and from there to the beer tent.

With his family around him, Paul is unable to react to the diagnostic news he has heard, though they seem to await his response. The conversation that finally begins skirts it altogether, except for Glenda, who continues crying softly.

Paul looks at his sister. For the first time, he registers, registering the change in her appearance. She is wearing a tartan plaid skirt with a pale green sweater and brown penny loafers. She looks distinctly like a woman and less like his sister. Only once does he remember seeing her dressed this way, when he saw the picture she sent him of her at McGill. Their phone conversations had always called up earlier images of her.

Paul asks his mother how she is managing with her diabetes and if her good friend Reba is still losing to her at hearts. He flatters her about her home cooking, contrasting it with the tasteless fare offered him in the hospital. He asks his father a series of question about the farm, its various machines, the livestock, the fields and fall preparations.

"Sure could use some more of those apples, Dad. The only real flavor I get in here," Paul says, smiling gamely. His father, too, manages a smile and a "Sure, son."

The conversation continues to orbit the grave news they have heard and finally ends with Paul's mother saying to Paul that, "whatever happens, we will all manage as we have in the past." Paul understands this to mean that he will be added to the burdens that they are already struggling to manage. His mother tries to hug him, but is constrained by the medical devices attached to him, so she kisses him on the cheek, setting her hand lightly on the new cast on his right arm. His father nods to him with a grave smile. Paul sees only his elongating eyelashes.

"See you soon, son; you take care. I'll bring some apples."

Glenda approaches him, making no effort to hide her tears. "I'll be back. She whispers to him. I'm just gonna see mom and dad off. Dad doesn't do well driving at night anymore. I think he's getting cataracts, though he denies it. I'm staying nearby. See you in a few minutes."

Paul is alone now with his prognosis. Strangely, he feels nothing about the news he has just heard. It is as if the radio has just broadcast news of a drought in a foreign country, eliciting in Paul an intellectual empathy for its victims. This emotional anesthesia frees his thoughts to return to his parents, both of whom appear strikingly older than he remembers them. He wonders if one experiences the passage of time as a chronological slide show of snapshots that only record intermittent change, like the eerie drawings he remembers in a Classic Comic book of Dorian Gray. He wonders if he, too, has aged in proportion to the aging he sees in his parents.

154

*Paul closes his eyes and tries to remember his parents at their youngest, but
the mental portraits he evokes keep changing, as if someone has dropped a
slide tray and replaced the slides at random. He sees Jolinda making out
with her lover. He sees Tommy watching the auctioneer empty his home.
He sees the seductive lemonade seller. He sees Theron removing a beaver
from one of his traps in the ice. He sees Glenda as a little girl stringing
rhubarb stalks in the kitchen with their mother. Gradually the inchoate
images become a dream that is a function of the glass bottle above his head.*

Paul wakes up in a mussed bed, suffering from a crushing hangover and
headache. He only remembers bits and pieces of the evening's events. He
knows someone is lying next to him and turns over quietly to see who. It
is the lemonade seller. She is lying on her left side facing him with her
left arm pillowing her head, as he has commandeered the only pillow. Her
ample exposed breasts are compressed horizontally in this position. He
recognizes the small scar on her right breast lying atop the other. Although
he is familiar with the body of the woman lying next to him, he realizes
suddenly, he doesn't know her name.

Lying still, he struggles to get his bearings and to recover the evening's
sequence of events. He remembers leaving the stock tent and going to the
beer tent. He remembers leaving the beer tent after a number of beers and
heading for the performance stage. He tries to remember whether he made
contact with Jo or just watched the band from afar. He vaguely remembers
her singing Roy Acuff's *Wreck on the Highway* and Patsy Cline's *I Fall to
Pieces.*

He is haunted by the idea that they saw each other and may or may not have
talked. His close-up photographic recall of Jo's girlfriend's face leads him to
believe that they must have met. He could never have limned such a specific
image of her face from the furtive sighting earlier at the merry-go-round.

He is struggling to remember how and where he met up again with the
lemonade seller. He looks at her sleeping next to him. There are pillow
wrinkles on her left cheek. He wonders if the musky odor in the bedclothes
is the result of their having had sex.

It is hard for him to comprehend that his countless imaginings and wet dreams about a first sexual encounter in romantic, almost sacred circumstances would so quickly have devolved into a coupling without memory. He is desperate for a glass of water and realizes that the rank taste in his mouth is not beer, but bourbon.

Unlike Jolinda's platform bed, this bed is a cotton mattress on open steel springs. He makes every effort not to jostle the bed or to make noise, first placing one leg on the floor and slowly rising.

When he first stands, he has to steady himself against the vinyl-paneled trailer wall as a wave of dizzying nausea sweeps over him. The trailer's bathroom is at the foot of the bed on the right barely enclosing a shower stall, toilet, and miniature corner sink. There is no drinking glass in there. He closes the door and takes a leak. His penis is sticky with the dry residue of sex, and his body is redolent with the stale smell of the sex he now knows he had with the stranger sleeping eight feet away.

He does not flush, but heads into the kitchen where he finds a dirty glass and downs two glasses of tepid, plastic-tasting water from an onboard cistern. On the counter is a woman's purse made of rough-out leather dyed pale blue with the remnants of some beadwork. Quietly he opens the purse and draws out a thin wallet. This he opens, looking for some identification bearing the sleeping woman's name.

"Alice," he hears coming from the bedroom at the other end of the trailer. She is standing at the foot of the bed naked and he suddenly understands that he, too, is naked.

Alice is smiling. "How quickly we forget," she adds wryly.

Paul realizes he is staring at Alice's nudity. He thinks again of his recent youth when his many dreams of seeing an attractive woman standing naked next to him were just that. This is not how he imagined it.

He grabs a dish towel and tries to cover himself. Alice giggles, telling him it's too late. She has already seen and tasted the subject of his modesty. Paul relents and smiles, saying, "I'm really sorry. I drank way too much."

"No need to apologize. It was fun. Your name by the way, in case you forgot that too, is Paul," Alice adds with a twinkle.

"Where are we?" Paul asks

"Still at the fair. This is my trailer. I'm a carnie. I travel with the concessions. My father and I used to travel together, but he died last spring. He was a roustabout mechanic, assembled and disassembled the rides. It's my trailer now. Want some more lemonade? You seemed to like the first glass. You came back.

"I did?" Paul asks. "Is it Sunday?"

"All day. Why? You're not a Bible thumper are you? You don't seem the type. You sure weren't very holy last night."

"I'm sorry if I did anything. I know I drank too much. I'm not used to drinking."

"Coulda fooled me. That pint of bourbon I pulled outta my pocket went down you like water," Alice laughs.

"Let's get dressed and have some breakfast," she adds. "You're gonna need something in that stomach to sop up all that booze you drank. Want some aspirin?"

"No, thanks," Paul answers, sniffing and pulling on his T-shirt and jeans.

Alice leads Paul to another trailer where food is being grilled up for the traveling people who make up the permanent contingent of all county fairs. She orders breakfast for the two of them.

The fat cook wipes his hand on his greasy apron and says in a French accent, "Well, well, Alice 'ave a new beau. What's dis one's name, honey?"

"This here's Paul. He works construction, met him last night. Nice guy. Make him one of your house specials. I'll have my usual."

Alice stakes out a vacant picnic table under the foldout awning and helps herself to two large coffees.

"Cream and sugar?"

"Cream, thanks," Paul whispers hoarsely.

Alice settles in next to Paul and slides a coffee over to him. "Breakfast'll be up in a minute. Julie's fast ... has to be when this place is hummin'. I've helped him out a couple of times. Not really enough room in that trailer for two with the grills and all. I've seen Jules short-cook fifty breakfasts in under an hour. He's been doing it for as long as I've been alive. He and dad were close."

Paul suddenly remembers his bike.

"Did it rain last night?" he interrupts.

"Not so's I saw," answers Alice. "Why?"

"Oh, nothing," Paul answers.

"You're thinkin' of that cool ride of yours. You were hell-bent on taking me for a spin, but I managed to talk you out of it. You started it up, woke up half of Dayton. Here are the keys. It's right where you left it."

"Jesus!"

"Yes, Jesus was with you, but I took you to bed."

Paul and Glenda are alone. Glenda is trying to collect her feelings after the shock of Paul's diagnosis so she can talk with him about what has happened, but her brother is strangely distanced from the news. Glenda decides to open with her news, though she fears now it will reverberate with Paul's.

"I'm majoring in nursing." Glenda announces, drying her eyes with a tissue.

"It's not like it was when we were little and had our tonsils out at Newport Hospital," she continues, "all those candy stripers skittering about, emptying bedpans and dispensing medicines. It's different now. Registered nurses can do a lot of things that only doctors could do back then. It's a real

career. I thought about medicine but, given the state of the farm, I need to be working sooner. Not sure how long mom and dad are gonna be able to manage the place."

Paul speaks slowly with his eyes closed. "I wanted to take it over one day and let them live out their lives there—add to the herd, do some beef, apples, firewood, syrup, and eggs. Can't do much in a wheelchair. Wonder if you can get 'em with flotation tires, bucket loaders and four-wheel drive?" Paul asks with a faint smile.

Glenda begins crying again.

"Don't cry, sis. I'm gonna need your help," Paul whispers. "I can't do this without you."

"I know," she says. "I just don't know how to help. I've learned so much in my first semester. We're already doing rounds at the Royal Vic, our teaching hospital. It's exciting. I'd no idea how much nursing had changed."

"I won't need a nurse," Paul says quietly.

"I don't mean that," Glenda agrees.

"I know," he says. "I'm sorry. I need to sleep now. Don't wait around. I'll probably sleep for another day at least. Mom and Dad need you more than I do. They're living in a dream world. I think they've been living on nothing. I've heard milk checks now barely cover property taxes. You should see the farms in the Midwest. They're milking 200 to 500 cows and still can't make ends meet. How can dad hang on, milking 35 girls? They'll have to sell the farm now. I can't ....Glad Uncle Theron ... Tommy?" Paul's voice trails off.

Glenda's sitting on the bed now and holding Paul's broken hand. Her cheeks are still damp from crying. She sees that her brother has gone back to his dreams and wonders what he dreams about. She does not know about Jolinda or the encounter at the county fair. He will tell her of these things in time, but not now.

Glenda can't foresee how her brother will cope with immobility. She remembers how hard it was for him to sit still in grade school. She recalls his voice compressed through a telephone wire trying to explain to her why he had to leave college.

Glenda, too, is tired. She kicks off her loafers and swings her legs up onto the bed beside Paul. She lays her head down next to his and drops into a deep sleep. Their dreams don't cross.

Paul is riding north on I-75. The onrush of fresh air clears his head, if not his mind.

He apologized to Alice, who seemed only too happy to have made his acquaintance. She wrote her name and general mail box address on the empty corner of a magazine page, though she warned him that she only was able to get her mail a few times during the year, and never was in one place long enough to hook up a phone. She asked for his number, but Paul lied, saying that his landlady had no phone either and he was not allowed to accept calls at the jobsite. Her parting kiss had seemed like an invitation to future foreplay, while the kiss Paul returned resembled the kiss he gave his mother when he left for college.

Paul is angry with himself that he can't know what happened the evening before and that he will be seeing Jolinda with no clear memory of having talked with her the night before.

Paul scans the horizon for troopers on the flat highway northbound, southbound, and in the bijou rearview mirrors mounted on each side of the apehangers. Seeing none, he opens up the throttle. He can only judge his speed by the flow of adjacent traffic. He has never experienced such response from a motorcycle. Danny's Vincent was built for speed, while Paul's chopper is built for torque. When he edges the throttle slightly, the large V-twin roars him by two fifty-foot semis in just a few seconds. After a few minutes of joyriding, Paul eases back to the speed of traffic and savors the panoply of landscape smells.

Home in just over two hours, he pulls into Jolinda's, kills the ignition, and walks the bike into the attached garage. Jolinda's truck is parked behind the apartment. He knocks on the door at the top of the stairs and then opens it and announces himself. The woman whose voice he heard at the merry-go-round talking to the little girl answers, "Come on in, we're here."

Paul's first thought is to leave as he had done the day before, but the mystery of Jolinda and her friend overwhelms his discomfort and he enters. Jo jumps up and rushes him, giving him a welcoming kiss.

"This here's Annie, she's my friend. You probably don't remember, but you met us last night with your friend, whose name I don't know 'cause you never introduced us. Cutie pie ... said she was a carnie."

Paul is lost. Annie's voice and face are as familiar to him now as they were when he woke up next to Alice.

"Probably don't want a beer," Jo laughs.

"I drank way too much last night. I've never had that much to drink. I hope I wasn't an asshole."

"Not too bad, but all is forgiven. If I'd known you were coming, we could have had some fun, the three of us. Annie is my other lover. As you've figured out, I'm a switch-hitter, but Annie and I go way back; she's just back from a trip out west."

"Was that her daughter with you?" Paul asks.

"Yes, we took her to the fair, she's back now with her asshole father in Cincinnati. Ginny's a sweet kid. No idea how she'll turn out living with that asshole. Hope he's not pawing her."

Paul doesn't know what to say or how to react to what Jo has told him about herself. He doesn't understand how, or if, he fits into her life now that Annie is there.

He says that he's made a Sunday dinner date with Mrs. Benton and has to change and head out soon, having promised to be there at five.

He retreats to the bedroom where he gathers his few things, and then sets his small duffel quietly outside the front door. He returns to the living room where Jo and Annie are sitting apart on the couch. He has lost his bearings and his words.

"Are you okay?" asks Jo.

"Just hungover," Paul answers.

"I should head out. Nice to meet you, Annie. How long you here for?" Paul asks with feigned insouciance.

"I have to be back out west for my next job by the fifth of next month, so I'll probably leave in two or three days."

Paul answers only, "Oh," and heads for the door. "Take care," he says and descends the stairs.

To his surprise, Jolinda is waiting for him in the garage. He is confused until he realizes she must have come down the wobbly fire escape behind the garage.

"Don't go away mad. You don't understand," Jolinda says, smiling.

"What's to understand?" Paul says. "You're homosexual. Some of my best friends are homosexual."

He surprises," surprising himself with the spontaneous reference to Tommy.

"I'm bisexual," Jolinda corrects, "and I meant what I said about loving you. You're one of the kindest men I've ever met. I'm sorry if this hurt you, but unlike you, I've never lied to you about anything."

"What have I lied to you about?" Paul asks surprised.

"You're not a liar. You're so damned afraid of hurting my feelings that you pick and choose what you tell me about who you are and what you're feeling. And even then, you bend the truth not to upset me. I'm not talking about the girl you were with last night; that means nothing to me. I'm no china doll. I'm a grown woman. I can handle the truth. I've handled more truth than you'll ever want to know. You haven't talked to Mrs. Benton for weeks. You're going there to escape me and Annie. It's okay. You never have to lie to me. I love you. I can handle whatever you tell me. You don't yet know or believe that about me, though."

"I don't know what I feel," Paul says looking away.

"Go, have a nice evening with Mrs. Benton, but come back. Annie's in Cleveland on business this weekend and we can talk. I'll roast a chicken."

Paul nods and begins pushing his bike out of the garage. He opens the fuel line, turns the key, pumps the starter to compression and jumps. The bike roars to life and he leaves.

Jolinda watches him, sees his duffel bungeed onto the passenger seat and knows she'll never see him again.

When Paul wakes up the following afternoon, he is grateful to be alone. He can't raise the energy to accommodate his family's empathy. He knows they are as confused as he is. Paul has never heard of the Kübler-Ross stages of grief. A therapist in the hospital will try to explain the progression to him, though they will mean nothing to him. Paul has long since known and accepted his outcome. Helping his parents through their own grief about his condition feels to him like more work than he can manage.

He recalls an incident at the Lancaster Fair across the Connecticut River in New Hampshire, where two summers earlier, he and Glenda had driven over to see the draft horse pulls. They arrived early and went to the grandstand area where the pulls were scheduled for later in the afternoon. They were surprised to see a groomed rectangle inside the race track oval with a mix of bay, sorrel and chestnut mounts with undersized saddles and riders dressed like English butlers milling around outside the groomed area. It looked like the start of an English fox hunt they had seen in the movie Tom Jones.

As they took seats in the empty grandstand near the front on the ground level, some chamber music began to play and the first rider reined her mount into the performance area. The erect riders seemed to be subtly urging their horses through a series of gaits, turns, and sideways-walks, all relative to markers on the field's periphery. A panel of similarly dressed judges watched and took notes on each horse and rider's performance.

Glenda and Paul discussed with one another what might be being judged in the competition, the purpose of which eluded them. The hand-lettered poster on the nearby fence simply said "Dressage Competition, central arena—2:00 p.m."

The sixth rider was a young woman mounted on a striking white Andalusian stallion with a tightly braided mane and perfectly combed-out tail. At first, her horse seemed reluctant, prancing in place until the music started. Then, as if suddenly released, the white horse entered the arena in an extended trot and began the series of moves with which Paul and Glenda were becoming more familiar. Suddenly, a roar of feedback accelerated through the PA system from an open mike near the sound system and the stallion reared up and bolted, throwing his rider to the ground.

A nearby groom chased and caught the stallion's loose reins while several other riders ran to help the thrown rider as Paul and Glenda watched from the grandstand. The rider seemed frozen in a half-seated position on the ground. She began frantically waving away the three riders trying to help her to her feet.

"Don't touch me," she yelled. "Call an ambulance."

The Caledonia Messenger carried the story several weeks later. In what for riders is a much-feared accident, this woman had understood instantly that she had broken her back and would never ride again.

Splayed on Route 100, before he first heard the distant wail of the siren coming to his aid, intimations of the depth of his injury had already taken hold in Paul. The painful succession of movement, surgeries, and convalescences only now confirm what Paul understood as he lay in an impossible posture on the cold pavement.

Mrs. Benton is delighted to see her former lodger even though she has had no advance notice of his visit. She had had to ask her last lodger to leave, as he was far behind in his rent and, on multiple occasions, she had heard the headboard in his room banging against the plaster and lath wall. Mrs. Benton is not a prude and knows full well that some men and women take any opportunity to couple. She just does not want it happening in her home. She expects little of her various lodgers other than the observance of basic proprieties.

Earlier in the day, Mrs. Benton prepared her signature shepherd's pie for herself and a widower friend of her late husband, who had taken up the habit of joining her for Sunday dinner. There are plenty of leftovers, and the smell of them warming in the oven makes Paul aware of his hunger. He has not eaten since the bacon, onion, and tomato omelet he forced down with Alice at the fairgrounds.

Paul puts his duffel in the familiar room with its ironed sheets and doily-covered dresser. He surprises himself in the gimbaled mirror and pauses to look at the man staring back at him, almost as if he is a stranger. He wonders whom Glenda will see when he gets home for Thanksgiving. He thinks about his friend Tommy and worries that he has become a pariah.

The construction schedule at this jobsite ends with the construction season and Paul will soon be out of work and on his way home. His headache has ebbed during the ride home and he is left only with the lassitude of his excesses.

After combing his hair, Paul joins Mrs. Benton at the table where she fusses over him as if he were a long-lost son. The order of her home and rectitude of her demeanor sit in stark contrast to Paul's memory of the profligate weeks he has spent with Jolinda.

After supper, he clears the table and offers to help with the dishes, but his exhaustion is apparent to Mrs. Benton who knows not to question him about his time away. She knows young men must grow up and do so in different ways. She gives him a goodnight kiss on the forehead, and sends him off to bed at 8:30.

The next day most of the heavy equipment is gone from the jobsite except for a small 'dozer used for light grading. Roofing and siding cover all 28 houses and only interior finish work and landscaping remain.

Paul is assigned to follow the 'dozer and hand-rake the graded topsoil around the houses. Workers carrying in the last sheetrock and appliances use the concrete entryways. Paul is surprised by the finesse with which the 'dozer operator, in spite of the machine's heavy tracks and blade, levels and grooms the landscape until he sees that the final passes are all made in reverse and the leveling blade smooths over the scarifying marks made by the 'dozer's tracks.

As the days shorten, Paul rakes, seeds and hand-spreads shredded straw over the soon-to-be lawns.

The following week, he arrives at work chilled by a noticeably colder fall morning. He has seen the dew on the lawn as he walks his bike away from Mrs. Benton's so as not to disturb her. Entering the worksite, he rides past another flatbed trailer parked at the entrance to the jobsite with a forest of identical, bagged and balled, triple-trunk, white birch clusters. It strikes Paul as odd seeing this rectangular glade growing out of the trailer.

A squat but articulate skid steer unloads and deposits a single birch cluster in the same spot on each lawn that Paul has recently seeded. Paul tries to envision the finished look of this vacant neighborhood. He has seen engineered neighborhoods only in Ohio. The random hill farms in northern Vermont bear no hint of any collective design. Houses, barns, and sheds sprout like countless mushroom varieties along the valley hayfields and dirt logging roads penetrating hillside forests.

Nor do the odd-lot mix of colonials and Victorians lining the elm-shaded streets of Vermont's small merchant towns exhibit any common architecture.

The development where Paul has spent his summer working reminds him of pictures he once saw in Look magazine of the modern row-housing built for British factory workers in the suburbs of sprawling industrial cities. He can't imagine choosing to live that close to a neighbor. He wonders what his Uncle Theron would say about such a neighborhood and recalls his telling their father his criterion for living on a plot of land.

"I'd 'ave to be able to take a leak anywhere within a mile of my cabin and not worry about anyone seeing me, 'cept a whitetail or a barn owl."

The following Friday, Paul goes to see the site boss to give his two-week notice. The burly Midwesterner pours him a mug of coffee and invites him to sit.

"You're from Maine if I remember right," he says.

"Vermont, actually, sir," Paul corrects.

"East of Erie, PA, it's all New England to me," he says with a smile, as he lowers himself into an oak-slatted office chair that creaks ominously under his weight.

"I'd kill to hire more guys like you. I can't offer you any work over the winter, except indoor painting down in Columbus, but if you wanna sign on again next April, I can pay you more and keep you busy earning good money until November again. Hell, bring a friend, as long as he works like you. I got a brother down in southern Ohio who builds developments. If he needs sixty guys, he's gotta hire seventy. People just ain't used to workin' anymore. I seen you was different. How 'bout it? Wanna work next summer? Give you an advance right now to come back. Ya stiff me, ya stiff me; but I don't think you're that sort. Fact, I know it. Well whatta ya say?"

Paul thanks the foreman for his trust in him, but explains that his uncle has left him a place to live and that his father needs help keeping up the farm. The foreman looks disappointed and rises to his feet.

"Here's my card. It's got my home phone number on it. I don't have no permanent office 'cept this here trailer. You wanna work? You call me anytime. Come see me 'fore you leave. Now off to work."

Paul closes the hollow aluminum door to the trailer. He is pleased and surprised by the foreman's appreciative words, especially as he has seen some men whose goal it is to avoid as much physical work as possible and stay employed.

On his last day, the foreman hands Paul $100 in cash when he leaves. Paul thanks him but explains that he can't accept the money, as he is not sure he can come back in the spring. The foreman explains that it isn't a deposit on future work, but a bonus for work well done. Taken aback, Paul thanks him. He shakes his hand and takes one last look at the houses he has helped to build.

His last night with Mrs. Benton is difficult for them both. Mrs. Benton's affection for Paul comes with no judgment. Her home has been a refuge for him and her unqualified affection has been as sustaining as her home-cooked meals.

Glenda is scolded by the charge nurse who wakes her from her nap next to Paul. The nurse says she will have a fold-down chair brought in should Glenda wish to spend the night with her brother. Glenda thanks her coolly. She must return to McGill the following afternoon for three days' worth of exams before she can come back to the farm for Thanksgiving. There is no plan yet for Thanksgiving since Paul cannot be moved except by ambulance.

Paul stirs but does not wake up. Glenda watches her brother intently and tries not to think about how he will cope with his future. His sporadic facial twitches and rapid eyelid movements betray his active dream state.

When he wakes, he tells Glenda that he had been dreaming about Tommy and wonders how he's doing. He tells Glenda things he has never told her before about growing up with Tommy and the early intimations of his homosexuality. He does this in such a way that she will understand that what they experienced together was not sexual, only that he comforted Tommy several times as his family continued to unravel. Glenda knows this and is amused by her brother's effort to distance himself from the simple kindness he showed his best friend.

Tommy tried to join the army, Glenda tells him, but his increasingly effeminate speech patterns betrayed him and the enlistment officer asked him point blank if he is a homosexual, which Tommy then admitted, as he knows it's a serious offense to lie on an enlistment form.

He later finds work at Corkins' Hardware as a stockboy. He is confined largely to the warehouse rooms in the back, maintaining inventory and restocking the shelves in the store after closing time. Mr. Corkins does not want Tommy in the store itself, perhaps afraid that Tommy's increasingly fey demeanor might cause embarrassment to customers or worse, that he might importune a customer. After several weeks in Mr. Corkins' employ, Tommy comes to understand that, in exchange for being offered a job, he is expected to perform certain sexual favors for Mr. Corkins among the barrels and boxes deep in the warehouse, so he quits.

Paul is saddened by this news. He has never known a homosexual and can't measure his sister's news against what kind of life homosexuals must lead. Glenda says that now Tommy does mostly odd jobs and that a few people in the community have come to accept him. Paul remembers his friend as a hard worker and recalls the many nights together in his father's barn working late into the night to help him finish chores.

Paul asks his sister if Tommy has anyone in his life, and she answers that, if he does, no one's heard about it. His existence at Theron's is remote and, as far as she knows or hears, he keeps his own company except when working.

In a tearful farewell, Paul separates from Mrs. Benton's hug. She hands him the $20 bill with which he has just settled his account with her.

"I have everything I need. You'll need this more than I will. Consider your last few weeks with me a gift for us both. I hope someday to meet the fine people who raised you. I believe we would have much in common."

"Please do come back and see me," she continues. "You have my address and phone number."

"Oh my heavens, I almost forgot! Your girlfriend called last night. You must have given her my number," Mrs. Benton adds, reaching into her dress pocket.

Paul freezes.

"She asked you to give her a call when you get home to let her know you made it home safe, and to send your address and phone. Seems like a nice enough girl. I'm glad you found someone to be with. Hope she knows how lucky she is."

"Yes, thanks," Paul says evasively. He pockets the neatly written note and the $20 bill.

Neither wants a long farewell and Paul goes through the short ritual of starting his bike and rides off east on the beginning of what will be a two-day ride home.

He had meant to have Hilger check out the bike before starting east, but did not have time. The bike has given him no trouble and he has twice changed the sixty-weight oil and regularly checked its level in the reservoir. The panhead doesn't burn any oil.

Paul is again on the road. He is anxious about arriving home. He has not been good about staying in touch with his parents and will now return without having finished his year in college. He is unsure of what Glenda has shared of their conversations together. He tries not to think of the discussion with his father and focuses on the open road ahead of him.

He is blessed with good weather, though it's cooling off considerably and he has made no plans for an overnight. The roar of the engine beneath brings a smile to his face and Jolinda's smile comes to him unexpectedly.

The orderly bringing in Paul's supper wakes him up. His long sleep and the barbiturate hangover have left him groggy. The opiate-induced agnosia that sometimes haunts him is diminished. He sees Glenda smiling at him. He nods away the orderly who sets the tray in front of Glenda and urges her in a conspiratorial tone to try and feed him.

To Glenda's surprise, Paul seizes on their time alone together to talk about his future prospects and plans. Anyone watching the conversation wouldn't guess the seriousness of their discussion. From time to time Glenda cries softly and shakes her head in seeming denial, but Paul's calm voice is persistent and doesn't exhibit the sadness that periodically overtakes his sister.

170

Glenda does not try to feed her brother. The pervasive odor of fried meat nauseates them both and she removes the untouched tray to the corridor floor outside and closes the door.

They continue talking together until dusk and Glenda again lies down next to her brother and kisses him farewell, promising to return the day after her exams end.

A taxi drops her at the bus terminal and, four hours later, the half-empty bus deposits her in Montreal within a few minutes' walk of her residence dorm on Rue St. Denis.

During the bus ride from Vermont, Glenda thinks about what Paul has told her about his time in the Midwest and his friendship with Jolinda. She does not see the relationship in black and white the way her brother does. She has come to understand that some women are more concerned about being able to trust a partner emotionally than about how they achieve orgasm, and that it is possible for them to express physical intimacy with whoever offers the best promise of reciprocating that trust. She knows, too, that most women will want children in time or have inculcated in them a deep fear of heterodox relationships and therefore will put up with much less in a partner than they might wish for. Her time at McGill has made her many new friends and several are women still unclear about their own sexuality, though only one eagerly talks with Glenda about it.

Paul is again sleeping and dreaming of Jolinda.

When Paul leaves the on-ramp to the New York State Thruway, he sits back as far as he can on the thin saddle and opens the throttle. For several miles, he passes every vehicle. Truckers often give him a horn blast or a thumbs-up as the throaty bike roars by on their left. Paul loves this feeling. The rush of wind from an open throttle in fifth gear and learning something new at work are his favorite experiences, though to his surprise, his recurrent flashbacks to his time with Jolinda also fill him with joy and sadness. He now regrets the implied judgment of his precipitous departure and thinks he may call her sometime.

Now at dusk, he is perpetually outrunning his high beams, going 65 miles an hour so he slows to 55. He is aware, too, that he's tired and the nine hours of steady road vibration have dulled his senses. He exits in Canajoharie, pays, and leaves the ramp headed east along Route 5 until he finds a dirt turnoff leading into woods. He follows the rutted road in second gear past several shabby farms until it dead-ends in a stand of tall white pines. He parks the bike, takes the small canvas tarp out from under his duffel, and puts together a makeshift sleeping bag out of the canvas and his windbreaker. He is hungry, but does not start a fire as he has nothing to cook and does not want to attract attention.

He sits down against the trunk of a large pine and just listens to the breeze riffling through the silvery green branches above. Small brown bats gyre through what little open sky he sees, gorging on flying insects. There is no sign of precipitation in the night sky.

In the morning Paul is rested and ravenous. He heads out, finds a small gas station along Route 5 and asks the proprietor where he might find some breakfast. The proprietor admires his ride and tells him of the shovelhead Electra Glide he used to own until his wife made him sell it.

"Just after I sold the damn thing, she left, and I was left with this place. Wish I had it back; I'd head out west. Don't miss her but I sure miss the bike," the owner says, tightening the gas cap and wiping up a few drops of gas on the tank with an oily rag he pulls from his pocket.

The proprietor sends Paul down the road about two miles to a local dinner where Paul orders a plate full of eggs, sausage, toast, and two cups of coffee for $1.99.

By 8:15, Paul is back on the Thruway with a new toll ticket in his pocket.

In the three ensuing days, Paul no longer responds to hospital staff. Dr. Abrams comes in twice and tries to engage Paul in a conversation about the final operation by a hand surgeon from Albany, a consult with the hospital psychiatrist, and his design for a program of physical therapy to restore the atrophied muscles that can still function. Increasingly alarmed that Paul is depressed, Dr. Abrams asks in the chief of psychiatry for a psychiatric consult.

Careful to give no sign of his attention, Paul listens to all that is said but does not answer questions. Dr. Milner orders a full psychiatric evaluation, but Paul has already made the decision to talk with no one but Glenda.

On the third day, his parents return. Paul wants to tell them how much he loves them, but can't find the energy. He looks at them, but his eyes do not follow them as they move around his bed anxious to elicit a response.

His mother looks old, though she is only 46. The once taut, tanned skin around her mouth and eyes is now translucent and rife with sun blemishes. He cannot see her swollen legs below the edge of the bed. She talks softly to him and he looks at her. She reads his demeanor as perplexed and says to her husband that their son "seems confused."

Paul's father is silent, but looks directly at him with what Paul imagines is pathos. Paul knows that the conversation he has dreaded for so long about his leaving college doesn't matter anymore. Perhaps the father, too, understands that his son has given up, as he too will later do. His father turns his attention to what he can see out the window in the parking lot below. Perhaps it is too hard for him to keep looking at the pale vacancy lying in front of him supported by hardware.

Glenda returns on the fourth day. She sits down next to him on the bed. It seems to her that Paul has gotten smaller and there is more room for her to sit on the bed. When Paul feels Glenda's impression on his bed and smells her scent, he opens his eyes, but says nothing.

Paul likes to imagine they are again in their attic room inside the farmhouse and Glenda has again snuck into his bed. She is showing him a treasure they found near the stone cellar hole to which they often venture in the woods. The cellar hole, a place of shared discovery and fear, is home to several long, brown milk snakes that sun themselves on the remains of the rock foundation. Glenda has convinced her younger brother that they are there to guard the treasures underneath the crumbling rock foundation, one of which she is holding in her hand. The unrecognizable coin lends credence to her earnest contention.

Paul and Glenda talk, falling silent only when a nurse or orderly enters the room to perform some routine task or to check Paul's vital signs. Glenda shuts the door again after each person leaves and they resume talking. She is no longer in tears. Dr. Abrams has threatened Paul with another feeding tube if he does not resume eating and communicating. He is back on electrolytes, which drip steadily into him through an IV.

Paul has just turned north onto Route 100 and is now eager to reach home. The long ride is arduous. He worries that he may have gotten some bad gas outside of Albany, as he hears occasional sputters coming from the V-twin, although it gives no sign of stalling. He needs to make it home before dark. The filament in his headlight vibrates with road shocks and causes the pale beam ahead to flicker, adding to the chronic problem of outrunning it after dark. Far ahead he sees a strange sight alongside the road. It appears to be a roadside vendor, but, on closer look, there are some chairs and a large white sign he cannot yet read.

The night nurse is annoyed when again she finds her patient's sister has fallen asleep in the same bed as her patient. She looks at the two for a minute and decides to finish her rounds before she comes back with a chair for the girl.

The second time the nurse looks in, Glenda's arms surround her brother and, in a change of heart, she turns out the light and leaves with a smile.

It is 6:47 and the morning nurse has found the patient in the traction and partial body cast non-responsive and without a pulse and has initiated a galvanizing code blue.

His sister watches from the visitor's chair that has been removed to a corner of the room as three nurses and two doctors scramble in vain to resuscitate the patient. Glenda knows that Paul is gone as she was with him when he left. She knows their efforts will be in vain. She excuses herself to make a call from the lobby, as she does not wish to be overheard when she calls her parents.

CPSIA information can be obtained at www.ICGtesting.com
Printed in the USA
LVOW13s1537101013

356371LV00016B/1067/P

9 780983 485261